To

To

my Dear Friend Cris

AMELIA'S SECOND BREATH

TALES OF LOVE

Doris Mae Honer

Amelia's Second Breath

Copyright © 2017 by Doris Mae Honer

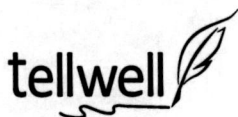

tellwell

Tellwell Talent
www.tellwell.ca

ISBN
978-1-77302-309-0 (Paperback)
978-1-77302-310-6 (eBook)

TABLE OF CONTENTS

ACKNOWLEDGEMENTS:

I WANT TO THANK ALL THE ADVANCED WRITERS IN "Words R Us" the writers group in the Juan De Fuca Recreation Centre, for their kind, knowledgeable critique that greatly assisted me to an improved quality writing.

Thank you also to my grandson Kirk Orth, for his input on how twenty-one-year-old young men would think and act. To my granddaughter, Jessica Orth, I am grateful for her wonderful photography. She inspired me to start planning the cover and to use her photography.

To all the members of Tellwell press' who graciously met with and inspired me to more advanced thinking.

Lastly, to my dear husband and friend, Ray Micholski, for patiently enduring my absence from him during the night and sometimes even during meal time while I disappeared into writing this story. He is a patient, serene, and loving man.

INTRODUCTION

AMEXLIA'S SECOND BREATH IS ABOUT A HARD WORKING Canadian woman from Saskatchewan and her life on the farm before and after the cruel death of her husband.

The book is alive with many interesting people, as well as historical events impacting throughout their lives.

It shows how every trauma brings its gifts, if a person is brave enough to take a step forward. Yes, sometimes this is difficult, but not impossible. One must be open to make new and better choices.

Sharing the load is essential, letting others help the afflicted person to rise is part of the story in *Amelia's Second Breath*

In turn, Amelia also helps herself to heal by helping an 8-year-old handicapped boy. She spreads her wings like a beautiful monarch butterfly, begins to make her own choices, and follows her own dreams and wishes.

This book begins in Canada's historical past, from the late 1890's, and continues again from the 1950's to 1970's.

Amelia's sister-in-law and dearest friend, Margaret, narrates the beginning of this lively story, and intermittently throughout the book. The people around Amelia, one coming from another

Canadian province, as well as her own wise actions, and how she begins to follow her dreams tell the rest.

My granddaughters Lena, Jaqueline, Lindie, Jessica and Hope, were insistent that I write my first book, *A Tale of Spirit…Yours, Mine, and Lessons from the Universe.* Therefore, I'm dedicating *Amelia's Second Breath* to all of them, who have faith in my writing skills, and in Spirit.

CHAPTER I

FROM THE JOURNAL OF MARGARET ARCHER

I AM WRITING THIS HISTORY MOSTLY ABOUT AMELIA AND Adam Archer, and the people in their lives, because their history is important both to me and to the little ones who come after all of us. My name is Margaret Archer. I write from the year 1920 to August 1, 1953, and then intermittently until 1974.

The winter winds of Saskatchewan blow hard on warmhearted, hardworking farming people. I know all about the people since I am one of them. My parents, Leonard and Alice Archer lived on a wheat field right next to the Hansen farm, since 1903. I was the youngest daughter in the Archer family and Amelia was the only girl in the Hansen family.

I have an older brother, Adam, who is a very funny, sometimes a pain in the butt "kidder," but he's a great help to my parents, and a good brother to me. He has shown a real aptitude for carpentry and mechanics ever since he was little.

There were two of us children left in our family. My baby brother got whooping cough same time as me and Adam did, too, but we survived and our baby brother died.

Whenever I could, I used to play with Amelia Hansen. She was the only girl, and had two older brothers. Our parents worked long hours during the day on the farm, so Amelia and I helped out most of the time. Amelia was a real good- hearted, kind friend, well loved by her parents, and my family, too.

The two older Hansen boys, Amos, and Jeramiah, helped their dad with the chores on the farm. They were twins, born in 1899, two years before the family moved to Southern Saskatchewan. That is when their parents, Joshua and Sarah, bought the farm outside of Moose Jaw. Sarah suffered one miscarriage, and the death a year later of a little boy who succumbed to the measles epidemic. Amelia and I were born in 1904, two years after that.

In those days, farmers' children were expected to help their parents with chores all the time, and all the farmers helped each other with the crops, husbandry, and everything else that would keep everyone going and surviving. We had some great socials, with lots of food to eat and fiddle music to dance to, and often the young folk were found kissin' behind, or in, somebody's barn. Amelia and my brother, Adam, got to know each other behind some farmer's barn at a social when they were in their early teens. Amelia's mom, Sarah, was good natured, patient and kind. She was a real good cook, too, and her bread always took first prize at the country fairs. She kept a close eye on Amelia and warned her against "doin' it" before marriage.

The year 1917 was a very sad year for the Hansen family. The twins, Amos and Jeremiah, had joined up to fight in the First World War. They were killed in action in 1917 just before the war ended.

Adam came often after that to help Joshua with the many farm chores, and to tease Amelia into loving him.

When Amelia was sixteen, her dad, Joshua Hansen, began constructing another house about two minutes away from theirs. My big brother Adam helped him build it. Joshua was a large, muscular man and very strong like a bull. When a tough job came up, the farmers in the surrounding areas could always count on him to help.

No one was surprised when the minister announced in church that Amelia and Adam planned to get married in August of 1920. It was a truly sweet wedding and farm folk came from miles around. The farm wives gave Amelia presents of quilts and bedding, tea towels and all. Each of the farmers had made some furniture for the couple, to give them a good help in starting out.

That wedding was the talk of the year! It lasted until the next morning, all that dancin' and singin'! But everyone had to go home at dawn to milk the cows and do chores. Some heads were mighty big and achin' by then, believe me!

Less than a year after the wedding, Amelia was showing a big round belly and we all started countin' back to the wedding with big grins on our faces. None of us was surprised, since Amelia and Adam had been a couple since they became teenagers.

That's part of the history of this story.

In March of 1921, Amos was born, and in the next 3 to 4 years, Jonah, Jeramiah and Sarah followed Amos into the family.

In 1924 Amelia decided she would change two of the biblical names, and Jonah became John; Jeramiah was shortened to Gerry. Her baby girl was named Sarah, and Amelia left it to honour her mother. Amos was already used to his name, so she let him keep it. Since her dad had insisted he liked the name John far more than Jonah, and would have preferred to be called John; it was too late, for he was always known as Joshua. He made Amelia promise to change any baby "Jonahs" that came along to baby "John." Amelia complied when she changed some of the children's names.

Shortly after Adam and Amelia had their last baby girl, which now made a family of three boys and one girl, her dad Joshua got real sick with pneumonia and died in April, 1924. He left a will. The farm and land were granted to Amelia and Adam, and they were to care for their mother Sarah for the rest of her life.

We farm folk were not great on schooling in the early days of the 1900's, since it took all our time to do farm work and grow wheat. Apparently, Joshua was schooled some in the old country and taught his children by candlelight at night. Amelia was real smart in reading, writing, and arithmetic. I was lucky and got schooling enough to become a nurse.

In 1928 Amelia's children were ready for school. She began pushing Adam to rent the farm because she wanted their children, Amos, John, Gerry, and Sarah to attend a real school in town. They moved into the town around 1929. Once the children were settled in school, Amelia applied to the local Business College and was accepted. Adam easily found work in construction, building houses, and later he found a steady job with the railway. It is interesting to note that the CPR (Canadian Pacific Railway) had been established in Saskatchewan as early as 1882, and brought pioneer settlers to Saskatchewan as late as 1931. The major communities had several trains a day heading out in every direction, transporting people and freight to almost every corner of this prairie province. Adam's growing knowledge in mechanics and eagerness to learn about trains made him a real asset to the CPR.

Amelia learned to be a stenographer and a secretary. Mother kept things going at home and was happy to cook, sew, and take care of the family. While the children progressed in school, Amelia found work first with an accountant and later at a lawyer's office. The children advanced in school and all graduated with good marks. Then each of them decided to leave home and seek their own fortunes.

Adam and Amelia worked for a long time until that horrible railway accident in 1946. It was winter, and Saskatchewan has some bitter- cold stormy winters, believe me. Adam and his assistant were fixing a jammed rail that had frozen shut at a crossing when the train approached without warning. Adam was knocked into the air and over into a ditch. The accident affected his back and paralyzed him. He had such a bad concussion that he was never quite right in the head after. Amelia cared for him until he died in 1950. He was only 49 years old.

Later on Amelia's mother Sarah decided to move closer to her favourite brother, Tommy, on Vancouver Island. She found a place to live in Victoria. Amelia's children were all finished school. The boys found work and went to live in other provinces. Young Sarah eloped with an American pilot who had been visiting Moosejaw on leave from his station in Alaska.

I've kept close contact with Amelia. After Adam died, I was overjoyed when she decided to move to Victoria following her mom.

Things seemed to go well for the trio until Amelia's mom, Sarah, just up and died of a massive stroke. That was in 1952. Then, to make matters worse for Amelia, her favourite uncle Tommy followed his sister in death. He had cancer and it became terminal. He died in 1953.

I live in Nanaimo and Amelia was in Victoria, so although we kept contact by phone, I didn't see her too often. It was the day I was preparing to travel to Ontario for a nurse's conference that I dropped in to visit with her before going to the airport. That was in August 1953, about a month after Amelia's uncle had died. When Amelia came to the door and let me in, I was shocked at the change I saw in her. She was emaciated, looked very depressed and certainly needed help.

I put a call right away to her second oldest son, John, in Winnipeg, Manitoba. It was difficult to reach the other boys because they lived in two different parts of the Athabasca tar sands in northern Alberta.

"Your momma needs help right away. You handle it, John. I have to fly to Ontario this afternoon otherwise, I'd be here to help. You take care of your momma!"

There was shocked silence before he responded.

"My God! Ella is in hospital having our first baby. I can't get away and both brothers are way up north in different parts of Alberta. They are both working for Alberta's Great Canadian Oil Sands project."

"Take care of it, John. I know you'll manage." I said to him. "I have to leave and catch my plane. When I get back to Victoria, I'll check on how things are."

We exchanged a few more words of encouragement to both of us, and I left to catch my plane.

CHAPTER 2

AMELIA'S CHILDREN
ARRIVE AUGUST 3, 1953

AMELIA WAS ONLY FIFTY- TWO. SHE LOOKED ABOUT 80 when I saw her. I can imagine what the sons would say when they got there. Amos and Gerry arrived at the apartment two mornings later, took a key from under the mat and entered Amelia's apartment.

"Mom? Mom! Jesus Christ, Mom! What's happened to you?"

Amos's tanned face creased with worry.

She was definitely emaciated. Amelia's usually attractive braided hair dangled in grey strands. A dirty apron covered a plain cotton dress that hung on her very thin body like a shroud. She had stopped eating. The usually spic and span apartment was dirty. Everything was untidy, musty, dark, and the whole place smelt of decaying garbage. She sat down in her rocking chair and looked out the window.

Their mother, whom they remembered as warm, vibrant, energetic and happy, seemed lost in a daze. What a drastic change from the woman they could always turn to when in trouble.

Gerry knelt down beside her, hugged her unresponsive little body and then put his head in her lap.

"Mom, what's happening? Look at you! What's going on? Are you sick? Talk to me!"

She stroked his head but looked away.

"Mom, come back to us. You gotta come back to us." He was sobbing.

Amos filled the kettle, put it on the stove and turned on the gas to make tea, then started washing the dishes.

They offered Amelia tea and toast which she nibbled at, then went back into her other world.

"My God! What are we going to do?" Amos was scratching his head.

"She's not herself. She needs help." Gerry was still on his knees beside his mom, patting her arm gently. "Let's call our sister! She'll know what to do!"

They talked about how she might be cared for but were at a loss for ideas.

To take her into any of their homes was impossible, since the sons were living in two different and isolated areas of northern Alberta. Their "one room" cabins were very primitive. There were no amenities or doctors up there.

Sarah, Amelia's daughter, was in Alaska with her military husband. Their facilities were sparse, consisting of two rooms and a bathroom. Their daughter was 3-months old. The brothers put a call to Alaska. Sarah immediately offered to come and bring the baby with her.

In the next few days, the sons cleaned Amelia's apartment, did several loads of washing, ironing, as well as washed floors and vacuumed every rug in the place. They restocked the canned goods, freezer and cupboards, made meals, coaxing their mother to eat.

Amos met Sarah and the baby at the airport three days later, and filled her in on the details while Gerry remained with his mother. He got her up and dressed her warmly. They walked together outside in the sunshine. Later he continued to clean the apartment, carting out more dirty stuff to the garbage. He cooked up meals, always sweet-talking Amelia into eating.

When Sarah arrived at the apartment, Amelia had on a clean nightie, dressing gown and slippers. Gerry had washed her clothes and Amelia looked much fresher and clean. Her facial expression seemed brighter with interest in her surroundings.

"Mom, how are you? I brought little Amy for you to meet."

Amelia responded with a vague smile. Sue placed baby Amy on Amelia's lap and Amelia looked down at her, took her little hand in one finger and smiled again gently. The baby began to fuss.

"Nice baby," she said and looked up at Sarah, as she handed the baby back.

"Mom! Amy is your granddaughter." Sarah expressed her exasperation and concern loudly. Amelia looked surprised, then pain crossed her face and she looked away. Tears began streaming down her cheeks.

"My God! What are we going to do?" Sarah looked imploringly at her brothers.

CHAPTER 3

TOUGH LOVE, AUGUST 8 - 12, 1953

IT IS SAID THAT IN VICTORIA IF YOU DON'T LIKE THE weather, and if you wait ten minutes, it will change. Sometimes I think that life there fluctuates as often.

My plane came back into Victoria at 10:30. Amos met me and filled me in on what was going on with Amelia. They had suggested to her that an assisted living place would help her, but she was adamant that she wouldn't go. She went back into her shell. The kids were desperate and time was a-wasting.

Amos and Sarah had scouted out the retirement homes in Victoria. They concentrated on the ones they could afford. I took care of the baby while they went to the Happy Days Retirement Home in Langford, close to where their mom lived. It seemed to be clean, the food palatable, and the staff friendly. It was the best fit for Amelia. There was one single room available. If they pooled their resources, they could afford it. Amelia's behaviour had been a combination of real deep depression laced with some caustic negativity and unusual memory loss.

She and I had been good friends since childhood, and sisters-in-law after she married Adam. I figured that since she was un co-operative with her children, it was time she received some tough love. Initially I spoke nicely with Amelia, and told her to accept any plans her kids had to help her. When she refused, I started the tough love approach.

"Amelia, be reasonable! Look at you! You've let yourself get so skinny! You need help to get better! I don't think you'd like me coming down and bullying you into cooking, keeping your place spotless and doing the laundry, ironing, taking out the garbage, getting groceries, making your bed, doing dishes."

I took a big breath, came a step closer to her, looked her straight in the eye again.

"Besides all of the above, you haven't made any friends, you know."

I then warned her that if she didn't co-operate with her children, I'd be visiting her often to keep on nagging her. I guess she thought about that because she snapped, "All right, Margaret! I'll look at the place, so stop bugging me!"

Her kids arranged a meeting with Ms. Betty Armstrong, for August 9. Betty was the Director of Nurses in Happy Days Retirement Home. Amelia came along, too, and seemed more than a little interested. They were all interviewed.

Miss Armstrong met them and cordially said, "Please call me Betty." She shook everyone's hand warmly and invited them into the office lounge, reserved for family meetings.

Amelia stubbornly refused to take part in any conversation or to answer any questions posed by Betty. The kids explained the circumstances in which they came to Victoria and their deep concern over their mother who seemed to be in a deep depression.

"She's depressed and acts a little funny at times." said Gerry.

Amelia gave him a nasty look.

The family said they would cover any financial concerns but that their remoteness and isolated lifestyle would not be conducive to her regaining her health by going to their homes at this time.

Betty was surprised when she learned that Amelia was only 52.

"We usually only take people in the home 55 years and older. With a twinkle in her eye she added, "She certainly looks a lot older than 52.""

Amelia had been sitting quietly, apparently not hearing anything, but she cringed when Betty commented on her age. Betty observed Amelia's reaction and smiled a bit more. She called the secretary to take down all the details, financial arrangements, and the signing of the consent papers.

"Don't worry, Amelia. We'll take good care of you." She said as she left.

After all the required arrangements for Amelia's stay were made, the consent forms signed, they were invited to have coffee in the resident's sitting room.

"Mom, I think we've done the best thing for you," said Amos who looked both tired and relieved.

Sarah agreed. "When you're better, either stay here or move out, whichever you want."

Upon their return to Amelia's apartment, we were all pleasantly surprised to see Amelia take Amy from my arms, cuddling her, making her smile and coo. She seemed more relaxed than any of us had observed her since our arrival many days ago. The family settled in, stressing to their mother the benefits of moving to a retirement home where meals would be provided on a daily basis, yet she would still have the freedom to go out to whatever activity she wished to attend or to go shopping.

"Don't you think I'm all right in my apartment?" Amelia snapped "I know I'm lonely here, but maybe that'll change when I feel better."

Amos, beside his mom, took her face in his huge hands.

"You've brightened up a lot since we got here Mom but I gotta say, you were in a real bad mess. This place was so dirty. It was like a pig pen, and you looked like you were starving."

Gerry added, "We all think you need some help to get back on your feet."

Sarah took back her baby from Amelia and jiggled her up and down. The baby gurgled and laughed. Sarah turned to face her mom. "We have to leave soon. Then you'll be alone again. Will you make your own meals and do all your own housework again or will you sink back into that awful hole you dug for yourself?"

Then she grinned, looking at me with a sly wink. "In the home you won't have to put up with Auntie Margaret bossing you around."

Amelia sat very still. Sighing, she said, "I don't want to change. But loneliness really hurts. I love seeing you, Margaret, but stop being so bossy! You give me a pain in the you know where."

On August 10, I had to drive to Nanaimo and it was getting late. I interrupted the chat by adding in my two bits again.

"Amelia," I said in my best overbearing voice. "Do I have to repeat myself? Please be reasonable! For Heaven's sake, help out your kids. They only wish the best for you and so do I. Your family has travelled a long, long way. They are very concerned. We all want to help you."

Amelia shrunk down in her chair so I softened my voice. " When you're better, you won't have to stay in the home. You can rent your own apartment again, or do whatever you want to do on your own. Maybe come to Nanaimo. Who knows?"

"This way, *YOU* will be helping you."

I said my goodbyes to the kids, gave Amelia a kiss, and on my way out I heard Gerry say, "Mom, we can decorate your new room with some of your furniture and pictures. You've got to help us choose what you want to bring with you, Mom." He put his arm around her and steered her through the apartment.

Amelia said, "If I decided to go, I'd choose some of the things I really love." They selected her desk and chair, the gooseneck lamp that had given her light for so many years, and Adam's blue stuffed chair with the footstool that sat on a flowered light blue rug.

She admitted, about his chair, "Sometimes I almost think my sweet Adam's sitting there looking at me." Then she added his tall brass lamp behind the chair.

"I'll be wanting to sit on my rocking chair, of course. I rocked all you babies in it for years, but I'm not promising anything, you know."

"We have to go home soon. We've got to move her." The children made the master plan. Before the appointed time that Amelia was to enter the retirement home, Gerry reserved a moving truck. Her furniture was to be delivered in the early morning to the room they had reserved for Amelia.

On that prearranged day on August 12th, 1953, while Amos, Sarah, baby Amy and Amelia were out for a drive, Gerry arrived very early at the retirement home. With the help of one of the home's maintenance men, they sent or carried all the selected furniture up to Amelia's reserved room. They busily arranged everything in a cozy, attractive way. I was included in their planning, too. The kids told me to call their other brother John, in Manitoba, and we planned the final touch.

After a long tour driving around town, taking in the sights in Langford and stopping at an Ice Cream Parlor, the whole family arrived at Happy Days Retirement Home. Both Betty Armstrong and Lori, the nurse's aide met them when they arrived. Betty and Lori took them around the home, which included a visit to the dining room, living room and activity room. Lori explained in detail about the activities and routines of the home. Lori had arranged many activities for the residents on her time off and was taking courses in night school to become a Recreation/Activity Director. She introduced Amelia to some of the residents who graciously welcomed her. While the family was touring, Gerry was finishing the last details in Amelia's new room and fussing impatiently. When the little group arrived, Amos opened the door wide. Amelia stared in amazement.

There was Adam's blue chair and stool sitting on the beautiful blue and flowered rug. The brass lamp stood gleaming brightly behind it. Her own rocking chair sat beside the window where the view looked out onto the small forest of trees beyond. Photos of her children and baby Amy were on the side table, near the small round maple dining table and chairs. A beautiful bouquet of flowers seemed to say "welcome" to anyone looking in.

Amelia caught her breath and stood silent for a moment, her hand on her heart. "I didn't think it would be like this."

Gerry came out from behind the door and hugged her in excitement.

"Mom, we made the arrangement anyway. It is something we had to do since we're all going away."

He smiled down on her face and kissed her cheek gently.

"We all want you to try it. We promise if you can't take the change after you give it a good try, one of us will come back and help you find something else."

While they were examining everything in the room, the phone rang on her desk. Amelia jumped a little in surprise. "Now who could be calling?" she asked with her hand again going to her heart. "There must be some mistake."

"Well, go and answer it Mom. It might be for you."

It was a long distance call from her second oldest son.

"Mom," John said, "I want to tell you something special. Ella had a little baby boy more than a week and a half ago. He was premature and for a while the doctors said the baby might not live. We didn't call you then. We were worried enough. We didn't want you worrying too. But our son is nice and strong now, and his name is Joshua, after Granddad."

Amelia gasped and sputtered how happy she was to have another grandchild, then passed the phone to Amos, who shared it with Gerry and Sarah, too. When they were all finished talking to John, they sat down grinning and chatting about the good news. Amos put the kettle on the two burner stove sitting on the counter, and took Amelia's tea cups out of the cupboard.

Amelia looked radiant. "I have a new grandson. This is the nicest homecoming present anyone could have given me. Would you believe it?" Still smiling, she hugged each of them. Then she picked the baby up and twirled her around.

The family knew that she had agreed to stay, even when she said, "She wasn't promising anything."

The next day, seeing that she was settled into her new home, they closed down her apartment, took her remaining furniture and most of her old belongings to St. Vincent de Paul Thrift Store. Then they returned to her room with a big box of Kentucky fried chicken and had a last meal with her.

"Mom, we'll be keeping tabs on you and visit you whenever we can get away." Amelia was now accepting the fact that she had to receive help to regain her health.

"I'll give everything you've planned for me a try." Then ruefully she added, "But I won't promise anything."

That familiar comment made everyone laugh. She had used it often when they were kids. She started to laugh, too.

Tears ran down their faces as they hugged and kissed her goodbye. Tears ran down Amelia's face as she watched her family leave.

I called Amelia later that night to see how she was doing.

She said, "You don't have to bully me anymore, Margaret, I gave in peacefully this time." She sighed. "I'm lonesome, don't know anyone."

I could hear a smile in her voice. "Come see me, but promise you'll be nice to me again. And bring me some chocolate." I smiled too.

Apparently, after we hung up, she went and sat in Adam's blue stuffed easy chair, leaned back, put her feet up on the foot- stool, yawned, and gently fell asleep.

CHAPTER 4

LORI AND AMELIA, SEPTEMBER 15, 1953

LORI, WAS THE NURSE'S AIDE WHO ADMITTED AMELIA. She was a round young woman in her early twenties with wavy brown hair tied back into a bun. Her sharp blue eyes and observant mind were quick to see changes and progress in her residents. Lori tried hard to keep the residents occupied; she knew that being busy and active was the key to maintaining good health and resilience.

Besides her day job in the home, she was earning a diploma in Recreation at the local college. She wanted to be a Recreation Specialist. On each of her shifts, she applied all she knew and the clients in the home looked forward to her care, which she supplied with much loving energy.

Lori came into Amelia's room to check on her and to make the bed.

"How're you doing Amelia?"

"I might as well do the best I can here." She grimaced and turned her head away. Taking a hanky from her pocket, she blew her nose. "My kids are all gone. I sure miss them."

Lori put her hand on Amelia's shoulder. "You are lucky. You have kids who love you and care about you."

"I know my kids love me. And I love them so much. Yes, I love them, but I wish I saw them more. They all live so far away."

Lori nodded as she walked to the bed and started removing all the sheets.

"They sure are worried about you. You have lost a lot of weight haven't you? Now you have to start eating to get better. Then maybe you might feel like visiting them once in a while."

Tears began to form in Amelia's eyes. She seemed very small, and somewhat frumpy, wearing a simple cotton dress much too big for her now, and an old pair of brown leather shoes. Her thick grey hair was tied into two braids pinned neatly at the nape of her neck.

Lori plied Amelia gently with questions. "Tell me about your mom and dad, Amelia. Where did they come from?" Very reluctantly Amelia began to talk.

"My parents were wheat farmers in Saskatchewan. Their parents were Norwegian immigrants."

"Norwegian immigrants. How come they landed in Canada?"

"They came in the early homesteading days, around 1876. That's when the Dominion of Canada's government granted them land in northern Saskatchewan," answered Amelia.

"Did your parents live in northern Saskatchewan, too?"

"No, when Mom grew up, she married Dad and they moved further south, near Moose Jaw. Dad was already established and was a wheat farmer."

Lori was putting the bedspread back on as she finished making the bed. She pulled Amelia's quilted blanket in the middle to make a butterfly shape at the foot of the bed.

Encouraging Amelia to talk, she asked, "Do you have sisters and brothers?"

"I was the only girl in a family with two older twin brothers. Many of Mom's babies died at birth or shortly after. There were only three of us left. My twin brothers helped my parents on the farm until they enlisted and went overseas during World War 1. I helped my parents work on the farm as much as I could, but I wasn't as strong as my brothers." She shook her head.

"Wow!" Lori exclaimed. "That was tough for your family. Did you go to school?"

"It wasn't easy. Dad tutored us by candlelight each evening when all the work was done. Both Mom and Dad wanted us to read, write, spell and do arithmetic."

"Did you ever have any friends, like maybe a girlfriend or a boyfriend?"

"I got along well with Margaret Archer, in the next farm from us, but I didn't see her very often. She was lots of fun. We were best friends and later sisters-in law."

"How about boyfriends?" Lori asked with a twinkle in her eye.

Amelia smiled a little, and her voice became soft and loving.

"When I was in my teens I fell in love with Adam Archer, Margaret's brother. He was two years older than me. I always liked him, even when I was little. Every year he'd come to help Dad harvest the wheat. He teased me but in a real nice way. He made everyone laugh.I always liked him and would tease him right back."

"And like a story book, you fell in love."

"He asked me to marry him when I was sixteen. My parents liked Adam. They asked us to live beside them on the farm. Dad and Adam built us a little house. Adam helped out with the farm work while he went to school in town."

"And you? What did you do?" Lori smiled.

Mom and I kept both houses and worked the garden. I started having babies soon after I was married." She smiled softly.

"What about your brothers?"

"My brother's names were Amos and Jonah, and they were good brothers to me. They grew up and enlisted in the military. I named two of my boys after my brothers. My boys even resemble my brothers."

"Where are your brothers now?"

"They were both killed in battle in 1917. It was awful when Mom and Dad got that news.

Lori bent and put her hand on Amelia's shoulder. "That would be terrible for your family."

Amelia nodded her head, looking sad. When my sons Amos and Gerry grew up, they went to northern Alberta. My second oldest son, John, went to Winnipeg. I used to hear from them all, but then they all got busy and I didn't hear from them."

Amelia shook her head. "It was out of the blue that both Amos and Gerry, and my daughter Sarah arrived to visit me. They said I was too skinny, and they suggested I move, so here I am."

"Wow. Amelia, you have quite a history! Ever think of writing your life story?"

"I hadn't, but that's something I might be able to pass on to my grandchildren. My granddaughter was here a while ago. I wish I could have seen her longer. Now my second oldest son John phoned and told me he and Ella have a son. They named him after my Dad." She smiled again, thinking of being a grandmother again.

Lori began to leave but returned for a moment and asked, "Amelia, was your marriage happy all the time?"

"Yes. I know sometimes we fell on hard times, but we always stuck together."

"Amelia, when I first saw you, you looked very depressed to me. You were and still are so skinny. I want you to consider something. Your body, your mind, and your spirit are all connected together, like in your marriage. Right now, you are here because you need help to become re-connected. You've been neglecting your body, and because of that, your mind and your spirit are both complaining."

She paused. "Adam's spirit must be very concerned when he comes to visit you. You've neglected yourself very badly."

Amelia looked surprised and a little stunned.

Lori continued softly. "You need to start eating more, and set things right for yourself, and your family."

"Let's say being here is your first step to you making everything right for yourself again.

We can garden almost all year round. There's quilting and a writer's group has started. Sometimes we go on tours, too. You might give these things a thought and let us know what you want to do." She bent over, kissed Amelia gently on the cheek and quickly hurried down the hall to help her next resident.

Amelia stood up and looked after her in amazement. Then she put her hand up to her cheek where Lori had kissed her.

CHAPTER 5

HAPPY DAYS RETIREMENT HOME, 1935 - 1953

BETTY ARMSTRONG WAS THE DIRECTOR OF NURSES IN Happy Days Retirement home. I knew Betty quite well, not only because of our mutual concern for Amelia, but also because we shared the same professional nursing positions. Often we met at meetings held in Nanaimo for the Directors of Nurses in various facilities within the province of BC.

Betty is a tall, slim Registered Nurse with long blondish brown hair always worn neatly fastened in a pony-tail or braided around her head. Her large brown eyes sparkle with both humour and intelligence. She had been divorced for over four years, and with part of the divorce settlement she applied and was accepted into University, where she studied psychology, gerontology, palliative care, amongst other subjects. She attained a bachelor's degree, majoring in psychology. Betty is well qualified to direct a retirement home. She is also a compassionate woman, fond of every client.

When we talked on the phone this week, Betty told me she visited Amelia several times. She kept me current on Amelia's progress. Neither of us agreed with Dr. Otto Burkhart's diagnosis, that Amelia possibly had the beginnings of Alzheimer's disease. We knew Amelia was very slowly showing signs of improvement from a deep depression. However, although Dr. Burkhart listened to Betty's observations, he was not yet convinced, and furthermore, he was getting very tired, lately. They were on good terms the doctor being very fond of Betty and greatly respectful of the many fine changes she was making in his retirement home.

Betty disagreed with him. "Otto, in my last course at university I wrote a paper on the many differences between Alzheimer's and Depressive Dementia. Our new client definitely fits into depression, is showing less and less symptoms of any dementia. She is coming along very nicely."

The old doctor grinned. He loved arguing with his Director of Nurses.

"That may be true at the moment, Betty. I know that Alzheimer's is a disease, while dementia is a group of symptoms. I studied the Alzheimer's disease in Germany where the first paper was written about it in 1906. There has been much more discovered since then, regarding the disease. Often people with Alzheimer's will show improvement when given proper care, temporarily. The same is true in dementia." Otto fiddled with his watch chain.

"Amelia was starving herself, and because of the three deaths of people she deeply loved, we could count deep depression as the only cause of her illness." Betty countered.

"I hope that is the case. I've seen too many young people with symptoms like hers to rule out Alzheimer's right now."

Betty shook her head in a definite no. Then she smiled and said, "Otto, I wish I'd known you when I was writing my paper."

Leafing through Amelia's chart, she showed Otto the graph she had made of Amelia's progress since day one.

"Look Otto, she was showing great memory loss and was at level 9 here. Now she's dropped right down to level 5. That's not Alzheimer's. It's an illustration of severe depression, improving in leaps and bounds."

Otto grinned even wider looking at the professional table she had made of Amelia's progress.

"God bless me, Betty! You're the smartest nurse I've met, except for Hilda, my wife. I'm awful glad you work for me."

His own physician had told him to slow down, because his heart needed medication to keep regular, and he was, after all, 76 years old. Twenty years ago he had bought the home at a very reasonable price, renovated it and turned it into an Assisted Living Retirement Home. He loved the home and the clients living there.

Otto Burkhart had three adult sons, Karl, Rubin, and Adolph. He appointed Karl and Adolph to take over the board, since they felt very capable of running the place. Rubin was away in Alberta prospecting and drilling for oil.

His grandson, Karl Jr., was a university graduate in accounting. Dr. Burkhart appointed him as the retirement home's treasurer.

While the board had run the home for the past twenty years, there were certain facts lately that made him feel very uncertain about the quality of care the residents were receiving. Therefore, he decided to establish a Registered Nurse as the Director of Nurses. Unbeknownst to anyone in the home, he had also hired his good friend Ken Michelson, who was a respected chartered accountant. He asked Ken to go over the books secretly.

His decision to hire Betty created quite a furor with Karl, the oldest son, who was the president of the board of directors, but Otto was adamant, and since he owned the home, the sons reluctantly agreed. Initially he had interviewed several RNs whom his sons had recommended, but he chose Betty on his own, when she sent in her resume. She was well qualified, and he liked her immediately when he interviewed her. When the board complained vigorously about her new ideas, he told them he was thinking of making her the new administrator, and they were to listen to her ideas. Karl was furious at this. "Dad, we don't need all her high-minded talk. We managed just fine before she came."

After working in the home for a few weeks, Betty sent in a request to both Dr. Burkhart, and the board. She asked them to consider hiring a Recreation Specialist. She included the salary to be paid and the required duties that would upgrade the activity level of each client considerably.

She also suggested that a dietician be contacted to teach the kitchen staff regarding the food. The menus presently offered needed alteration in order to serve more nutritionally balanced meals. The staff's methods of preparing the food required some improvements as well. The dietician could teach the kitchen staff to use a more sanitary method of kitchen maintenance.

She commended the kitchen staff for their hard work in the home but noted that they would benefit by more professional help to teach them to reach the new hygienic standards being set by the Department of Health.

The doctor thought these recommendations were commendable and said so. She had not heard from the sons on the board as yet, which irritated their father immensely. Betty was certain that there was quite a bit of money coming into the building through the monthly fees each client paid, as well as donations from appreciative families. She was also aware that several of the residents' relatives, who had died, had included ongoing donations to the home in their wills. She was determined to find out where the money was going.

CHAPTER 6

THE DOCTOR AND KARL BURKHART

THIS EPISODE I'M ABOUT TO DESCRIBE FLEW THROUGH Happy Day's Retirement Home like a wildfire devours Saskatchewan grasslands on a hot blistering summer day. I heard it through the grapevine, you might say. I wish I'd been a fly on the wall when this meeting took place! It happened that late September in 1955, when we were enjoying our gorgeous Indian Summer.

Betty was sitting at her desk thinking about what plan could entice Amelia to leave her room. The staff had tried several different approaches, but Amelia was adamant that she wished to stay in her room. The office door was open when a tall, handsome, broad shouldered man marched arrogantly into her office, strode up to her desk, slapped his big hands on her polished glass desk top, leaned forward towards her till they were almost nose to nose and snarled, "I'm Karl Burkhart. I haven't called you to a board meeting to meet you, but I'm Otto Burkhart's oldest son. I'm also head of the board here."

Betty quickly pushed herself away from the desk, stood up, and offered her hand. She responded in a level tone, "Karl! Nice of you to drop in. But you seem quite upset. What's going on?"

Ignoring her gesture, he, too, straightened up. "I don't know what you're trying to do, but whatever it is, it won't work. The board makes all the decisions and your ideas don't count around here, so get off your high horse, keep your mouth shut, and keep everything the way it is now." He smirked disdainfully down on Betty.

Although shocked, Betty maintained her calm composure. Taking a deep breath she said, "Karl, I don't know what you're talking about. You certainly appear distressed about something. Please sit down, so we can discuss the problem."

"No, I don't have time to talk to you. It's about the recommendations you gave to my dad and the board about improvements. You know nothing about how to manage a retirement home. The board has run this place for almost twenty years and it runs fine. We don't need any of your stupid ideas to rock the boat. If you want your job, keep your mouth shut, and do what you're told!"

Unbeknownst to either Karl or Betty, Doctor Burkhart had been walking up the hall when he heard Karl's loud voice coming from Betty's office. He stopped and waited quietly outside the office door.

When Karl had finished his tirade, he glared at Betty, turned on his heel and stomped angrily out her office, slamming the door shut. He immediately came face to face with his father. Shocked and speechless, Karl came to an astounded stunned halt.

"Son," Otto said very quietly. "We need to talk."

Putting his hand firmly under the elbow of an astonished Karl, he began walking, moving them both down the hall towards the exit.

"Let's go home and have a cup of coffee. Your mom made your favourite muffins this morning."

Gravely he added, "We need to straighten a few things out." The two tall Burkhart men headed out to the parking lot.

Unaware of what had just happened outside her door, Betty sat back down in her chair. "Whew!" She took some more deep breath, picked up her cup of coffee, noticing that her hands were shaking. Years ago she had learned to keep emotionally calm when faced with extreme anger and explosive emotions.

Aside from all she learned through courses on anger management in school, many years ago when she was still married, she had taken counselling to help her when her ex-husband exhibited similar explosive behaviour.

Keep calm, she told herself. She had also learned that the best response was to answer with a soft voice and step away from the line of fire.

The best reaction is no reaction, she remembered from one of her psychology lessons.

Betty put her head in her hands, reflecting on the moment, then got up to make her rounds. As she re-opened her office door, the phone on her desk rang.

It was her psychology professor, Bob Emerson, at the UVic.

"Betty," he said, "I wonder if you and your facility would consider being part of a trial project I've been planning."

"What do you have in mind, Bob?"

"I'd like to include you on the board as an advisor and want your input as the facility director." Betty sat back down, interested.

"Briefly, the plan is to see how interaction from our psychology students and the elderly in facilities would enhance the elderly's quality of living and give the students a better understanding of the need areas of the elderly. We would run the program for three months with frequent evaluations as the program progresses. What do you think, Betty?"

Betty's jaw dropped. She had difficulty believing her ears.

Bob explained his plan, stressing that there would be no cost to the facility for the program.

"I'm thinking of assigning one mature student from this year's third year. His name is Adam Wheeler, and he was a Canadian Armed Forces pilot in the Korean War. Would you have any resident who might be having a difficult time and could use some help? This is a confidential call, Betty. Names will not be repeated."

"Why yes, as a matter of fact, I do. Her name is Amelia Archer and she would be an ideal resident for Adam to work with."

Bob grinned. "Great," he said. "If successful, it will be run for all the third year psychology students next year."

They arranged to meet and go over details, settled on a time, place, and day. Betty was to contribute any ideas to enhance the project. Bob made some pleasant social conversation and they cordially said "Goodbye for now."

When Betty hung up her smile was as brilliant as a colourful morning sunrise!

I can hardly wait to tell Otto the good news, she thought as she began making her rounds.

CHAPTER 7

A FAMILY INTERVENTION

OTTO'S WIFE COMES INTO THE STORY NOW. I 'VE KNOWN Hilda Burkhart for a long time. We were both nurses up in Nanaimo. She is a wonderful lady, sensitive, intuitive, and very responsible. She was head nurse in the psychiatric unit then, and had both intelligence and knowledge as well as a good sense of humour. She married Otto after her first husband died many years ago. Together, they have three boys: Karl, Adolph, and Rubin.

Hilda is co-owner, with Otto, of the retirement home. I've met Karl the odd time. He always came across to me as impatient with anyone who disagreed with him or who wanted to change his own direction. He was a member of the armed forces in Africa, and had won a few medals for bravery. He'd been shot down over enemy territory but was lucky because he was rescued immediately by a Canadian reconnaissance team.

Hilda told me the following episode.

When Otto and Karl left the retirement home they went straight to the Burkhart's. Hilda spied them coming up the garden path and hollered out to them from the open kitchen window.

"You are just in time, fellas! The muffins are out, still warm and mouthwatering"

Karl and Otto trudged up the kitchen stairs, across the back porch and into the kitchen where Hilda greeted them warmly with big hugs.

Otto kissed her, mumbled that they would be in his office den having a business meeting. Karl slouched and went straight to the office.

Hilda looked at them intently, said nothing, and busied herself setting up a tray of steaming coffee and muffins.

Upon entering the den, Karl went to sit on the couch, and Otto chose a comfortable chair near him. Hilda bustled in with her tray to serve the men. She was thinking, *"What a surprise to see them this early in the day. I'm glad to see them anytime."*

After serving the coffee and muffins, she put the tray down on the desk, and sat down on the couch beside Karl. They sipped their coffee, while Hilda made small talk about the new bright blossoms coming up in the garden and that she had seen a robin that morning. As she chatted away, she observed both men intently.

Karl barely nibbled his muffin. Hilda nudged him. "Honey, I made these especially for you. I was about to call you to drop in when you and Dad came home. These are your favourites! What's going on?"

Otto took off his glasses, polished them carefully and without looking up said, "Mom, we have a very serious problem here, and it looks like the problem is Karl's actions and attitude."

Hilda took a deep breath and in a kidding way asked, "Karl, have you been shooting off your mouth again?" Karl winced but said nothing.

Otto put on his glasses, and grimly said to them both, "I'm afraid it's very serious."

Turning to Karl he said, "Hilda and I need to have a heart to heart talk with you, Karl." His oldest son Karl hung his head, began clenching his hands into fists silently. Hilda looked alarmed. The doctor continued.

"Karl, first of all, you had no right to talk to our Director of Nurses like you did this morning." He shook his head, and answered Hilda's questioning expression. "I overheard him having a *boss talk* with her, Hilda. You know what I mean."

Otto cleared his throat and turned again to Karl. "That's bad enough, Karl, but I've talked to our grandson about the treasurer's account."

Karl looked almost sick. Otto continued, "There are severe discrepancies in the accounting books." Hilda nodded, now understanding more about what was going on.

"Our grandson was very up front about your requests for money, Karl. However, the total of 130 thousand dollars is what you have taken from the home. You haven't paid anything back as you promised when you talked Karl Jr. into issuing cheques to you. What's going on?"

Heaving a big sigh, Karl said, "Mom and Dad, I had hoped to get everything back on the books before anyone noticed. I was having a tremendous winning streak before everything crashed. It hasn't worked out. The bottom line is I have gambled away what I took. I have to face myself. I have lost the funds gambling."

There was a long silence from both parents who stared at Karl in disbelief.

Then Hilda spoke. "How long have you been gambling son? When did all this start?" She put her hand on his arm gently, although her face showed absolute shock.

Karl answered regretfully. "It started after I went to that convention in Toronto about three months ago. I sat beside an old air force buddy on the flight back. It was good to see him after being away from flying for this long. He told me all about his winnings at the casino. He mentioned he'd won almost 5 hundred thousand and bought himself a condo out here. He gave me a few tips and I thought I'd try it. I was good at black jack back when we flew jets in Korea. We'd played cards when we weren't flying, and I always won." He sighed deeply.

"I thought it would be easy to win at the casino, and I'd surprise my wife with all the stuff she's been asking me to buy for her. I was doing well, but the bottom fell out and I'm now in debt up to my ears."

Hilda shook her head, "When Dad told me about his concerns, we called in our accountant, Ken Michelson, to check the books. Now that we've discussed all the ramifications of the choices you've made, I think we should call a council meeting with Karl Jr. and Adolph. We'll ask Ken Michelson to give his report. What do you think, Dad?"

Otto asked Karl, "Are you still going to the casino?"

"No, Dad. There's a list and photos of people they won't let back in to play, at the request of the person, and I put my name on the list."

Hilda said, "Good move, Karl."

Otto looked reassured but still very grave. "Okay, you have at least addressed your gambling habit. Good. It looks to me that you have two choices here, Karl. Either you intend to work with us on this or run away and leave us with this debt to solve ourselves."

"Mom and Dad, you know I'm not a coward. I don't intend to run away. I'm going to work it through."

"Great Karl." Otto sounded relieved. "I was very, very worried."

Shaking his head in despair, Otto continued, "Because if you chose to leave this situation and force us to go legal, we would have to take you and your son, Karl Jr., down with you."

Hilda was thoughtful before she spoke. "We know your air force record shows great bravery in the line of duty. You have always stuck to your guns when the going gets tough. However, this present situation has serious ramifications. Gambling is addictive."

In the silence that followed, Karl put his head in his hands. He said "Look, Mom, Dad, I said I wouldn't run. I told you I'd stay and work this out. I'm so sorry! The whole thing got out of hand! I intend to work it out somehow. I won't let the family down. I will work it out."

Otto went to sit on the couch on the other side of Karl. "Then if you plan to work it out, you will have to include us in the plans. We own the business. The problem now belongs to all of us. You will have to be prepared to do what we ask, and not try running the show yourself."

Rubbing the bald spot on his head, as was his habit when deeply concerned, thoughtfully, he then put a hand on Karl's arm.

"Here's what I've been thinking. The council will draw up a rough agreement as to how you will make restitution. Your brother can add his input before you sign it. I intend to make some changes in the board. Until you pay the debt in full, I am asking you to step down as president of the board. I intend to make Betty Armstrong the home's administrator; she will be part of the board meetings. Hilda will take over as president, and you will work with both your mother and Betty as a consultant. They will benefit from your many years' work here, running the board. But they will have the last say."

Karl gasped. "Your first step with Betty," Otto continued, "is to apologize for your words and behaviour this morning."

Now gulping and sputtering, Karl cleared his throat and pushed his dad's hand away from his arm, growling, "But Dad!"

"Karl, you have no further say in this matter."

"I can't stand that woman! She has taken over the home and thinks she's so smart." Karl shook his head, stood up, ready to walk out.

His dad rose and stepped in front of him.

"Karl, if you take one more step out this room, we will have you charged."

Karl sat down. Otto sat beside him. "The extent of the debt you owe is quite a sum. I want the home to receive a reasonable amount as soon as possible."

Karl's expression was somewhat belligerent as he leaned back, putting his hands behind his head and closing his eyes.

Otto continued, "You say you'll work it out. You will have to bite the bullet. You can count on our family's emotional support. I think you may have to put up with some comments from your brother, but it won't hurt you to learn to eat humble pie. Regarding re-payment, we suggest you work with Ken, our accountant. He can help and be discreet."

"Another thing Karl" said Hilda, "You must see a counsellor. You may not think you are an addict, but that is to be determined. I already know of someone, and I believe you will come out of all this a wiser and better man."

Karl took a deep breath and said, " Mom and Dad, call that family council meeting. I gotta say, it will be such a relief to rid this awful feeling. I will co-operate even if it kills me."

Much later in the day, Otto returned to the retirement home and was met by a smiling Betty. With new sparkle in her eyes, she related the call from Bob Emerson about the student coming from the university to assist the home for his project in psychology. Otto reflected back to her his thoughts about the psychologist's proposal. "If this is done properly, it will be a great boon to our residents." He was happy that they had wanted to use his facility, and counted on Betty's judgment to make this a real opportunity for his residents. When she asked him not to mention it to the board as nothing had been contracted as yet, he agreed. Otto felt relieved that something positive had occurred for the residents in his beloved retirement home.

CHAPTER 8

ADAM WHEELER, OCTOBER 25, 1954

"MARGARET, I NEED TO PICK YOUR BRAINS ABOUT AMELIA"
It was Betty, calling me last Saturday morning. Apparently, the
only time anyone could convince Amelia to come out of her room
was when I came to take her shopping or to go downtown. We
all agreed that Amelia seemed stuck. I thought Amelia was a
very angry lady, and couldn't express it. Getting her to talk was
like pulling bent rusty nails out of old hardwood. Betty said
that Amelia would be seeing a psychology student, and we both
thought it a great idea.

It was a beautiful October 25 of 1954. The trees had been
turning different colours of autumn, and frost was in the air on
some of the colder nights. Well over two months had passed since
her admission to the retirement home. Amelia was still in the
habit of sitting by her window staring out at nothing, when there
was a knock on her door. Amelia called out, "Come in."

A powerfully built man with curly brown hair entered the
room, closed the door softly behind him, and came to stand erect

at attention before Amelia, about ten feet away. He carried a three-ring binder in his right hand.

"Jesus Christ," he thought. *When I read her chart it said she was 52 years old! This lady is in her late seventies or early eighties! Someone must have made a mistake."* His face wore his shocked amazement, and Amelia caught it.

What's going on with him?" she wondered. *What is he seeing that I don't know?* She leaned forward; the rocking chair bumped the little table beside her and the flower vase of fresh flowers began to tumble.

In a flash, he closed the distance, grabbed both the table and the vase, righted them, turned, caught his foot on the rocking chair and fell flat on his face at Amelia's feet.

My God. He took a deep breath. *What a way to start an interview.* He sprang back up on his feet and back where he started in another second.

He moves fast like a cat and carries himself like a military man. Amelia looked at him with new interest.

Clearing his throat, he said, "My name is Adam Wheeler, and I am a student in the psychology department at UVic. I wonder if you could help me with a project I am doing." He stood very still.

"Thanks for saving me from picking up glass pieces and having to mop the floor." said Amelia as she looked closely at this young man.

She thought, *His name is Adam, and when he looks a certain way, he even looks like my Adam.*

Adam Wheeler was a man in his late thirties. After completing a stint of flying reconnaissance over the Middle East, he returned to Canada, resigned his rank of Captain and enrolled in the University of Victoria. His wish was to become a psychologist. He was married and had an 8-year-old son.

Amelia motioned him to come closer to her. "Nice to meet you, Adam. How can I help you with your project?"

Adam's shoulders relaxed and he laughed. "Well, Mrs. Archer, I was hoping to make a smooth professional entrance. Your doctor has given me permission to interview you and to learn more about you. I asked many questions about you before I came here. They must have made a mistake about your age."

"Yes, and you were expecting something other than what you saw when you first came in. Right?"

"Yes." He admitted with a grin. "They said you were only 52."

Amelia's face reddened, and her expression hardened. She snapped, "I am 52, young man!"

Oh crap. Adam gulped. Then thought, *tell the truth.*

"I was told of the many tragic events which have occurred in your life. Obviously, these events have made you appear older than you are."

"Let's get on with it, Adam. You may call me, Amelia. How can I help you?"

"I'm working on a study of the effect young people have on the elderly," he replied.

"That's not up my alley, anymore. The young people in my life have all flown the coop, so to speak. They're gone." Amelia said, dryly, shaking her head.

He started looking for a chair. "May I sit down somewhere?"

"Yes, over there." She pointed to the wooden maple table with two straight backed wooden kitchen chairs. When he sat down, the chair protested loudly and wobbled.

"Perhaps you could give me your opinion, since you are more mature, now, but you must have observed young people." He opened his binder while talking. "You have 4 children, don't you?" Adam seemed to become somewhat uncomfortable as to how Amelia was responding.

"Yes, and two grandchildren now. But like I said, they've gone their own ways." Her eyes flashed a little, with anger, and then with sadness.

"There are no more young people around me, anymore," she emphasized and clenched her fists. Getting up, she moved to the stuffed blue chair closer to him and away from the window.

"I'm a fairly young person," he said. Taking a deep breath, he added, "I'd like to get to know you better. I hope that's okay with you."

Before Amelia could answer, he continued. "When was the last time you saw your children?" Her expression reflected annoyance now. "I don't know," she said impatiently. "I think the last time was when they put me in this awful place and then left for their busy lives. I've lost track of when that was, exactly."

"I'll bet it feels lonely not to see them, doesn't it?" He spoke gently, with compassion.

Amelia stopped, and paused for a long moment, looking down at her clenched fists.

"It is very painful."

Adam's face was concerned and sympathetic

"Tell me about the pain."

She sat silent, thinking for a few moments then said, "I don't understand why loneliness and grief can hurt a lot, and can make a person sick. It is a very painful place to be." She wiped both eyes.

"Do you mind if I make some notes? Sometimes my memory isn't too accurate."

Amelia nodded, "Join the club about memory."

Adam wrote a few lines, added a question mark, then looked straight at her ready to ask another question.

She cut him off unexpectedly. "How old are you, Adam?"

"I'm thirty-nine, Amelia. Look, I'm sorry if I showed surprise when I came in. You've had a rough deal in life losing three of your loved ones so fast. It was horrible what happened to your husband, hard for you to take care of him for so long, and then to lose two more very important people in your family, one right after the other. They told me a bit more about it before I came up here."

He leaned towards her, speaking with much feeling."It's just that at age fifty-two, you still have your whole life ahead of you! Your people died on you, yes but, Amelia," He took a deep breath, "You're, still here! Think about it. Your kids are all grown and independent, because you raised them well. They sure cared about you because three of them came to attend to you the best way they could."

Amelia was concentrating on his words.

"But now! start to take care of you. Hey, make and follow your dreams. You have time to do whatever you want."

He started writing in his notebook, while the wheels started rolling inside Amelia's head.

"Do you ever phone or write to your children? And do they ever phone or write to you?"

"No." Amelia quavered. "They all work. They live in remote places."

"They all use a typewriter or write by hand." She opened her hands in complete despair. "I can still use a typewriter, I think, but since Adam got sick it's like I stopped progressing in the world, and now it's whizzing by without me." A tear ran down one cheek. "It's so frustrating." Adam was at a loss for words. He walked around the room studying the pictures on the wall and the one propped up on the side board.

These paintings are amazing.

"Amelia, these paintings are so beautiful," he commented enthusiastically. "Who was the artist? They're nor signed."

Amelia blushed. "I did them before Adam was killed. I didn't think they were good enough to sign them."

"Amelia, I'd swear they were done professionally. You certainly have a talent."

He went back to studying the paintings. "My project is to get young people and seniors together." He thought of his own son Ben, who desperately needed someone special to give him confidence, since the accident.

Why not get those two together? He thought as he examined Amelia's art. *The art would be bonding, and they both could help each other. Ben's a real artist himself.*

He turned to Amelia. "Would you like to help a young boy with a few of his studies? I mean my son. He's only 8 and has experienced a real trauma." He waited for her response. "I'm sure we could get him up here, so you and he could get to know each other. He sure needs someone to help him."

She looked puzzled. "Do you think a woman my age could help someone so young? I'm not even sure what to talk about to a child. He stood in front of her, with a slight pleading look on his face

"My son is in grade three. He started learning to type and knows his letters since Kindergarten. He is a good boy but suffering from the trauma of an accident. One thing he loves to do is sketch, and is amazing in getting likenesses right away.

"What happened to him?"

"He was on his bike, and was knocked over by a drunk driver. He's bright enough but needs some confidence socially, since some of his classmates make fun of him. He suffered some serious head and spinal injuries but has recovered from some of that. He's in a wheel chair. There are always bullies in school and he has an overabundance of them in his class."

Amelia looked at Adam intently, remembering how she had been efficient in working at the Saskatchewan lawyer's office when the family had moved to town. She remembered handling some tough clients. Her boss often said of her, "Amelia can always smooth any troubled waters."

Then she recalled all the art she had done in school and all the encouragement she had received to go on to higher education in art school.

It seemed so long ago.

Have I stopped dreaming? She asked herself. *Why I never thought that far ahead. Have I stopped learning? Gosh, have I been*

stuck grieving and being angry at my kids? But dreaming, learning new skills, teaching a little fellow how to cope with his own trauma, that's a great idea. Its a new beginning!

Adam stopped pacing, leaned on one arm of the blue stuffed chair, still enthusiastic. "We can bring Ben up in the elevator. We have some extra books and canvasses he can work on. He's really good at drawing. But he needs encouragement and support. We give him what we can at home, but some of his fellow students are merciless."

He cleared his throat. "I'm sure no one here in the facility would mind. If you want, I'll check it out and get permission. What do you say?"

Tears welled up in Amelia's eyes, as she pictured little Ben coming up to meet her.

She smiled for the first time in a long time. "Adam." Her expression was full of hope. "I would like to help your Ben. I know I can help him."

· · · · · · ·

When Adam returned home from school that evening, his wife, Karla, met him with a kiss and a hug, and then he went straight to his son's room.

He tugged at his son's shirt- tail. "Hey there, little Ben, I have a job for you if you want it, buddy."

Ben was working on a charcoal drawing of their dog. With his shirt- tails hanging out, he wheeled his tiny wheelchair around and blinked in surprise. "A job? What kind of job? Will I get paid for it?"

The subject of Amelia was talked over during supper, with Adam first explaining that the subject was confidential and not to be discussed outside their home. Adam carefully explained to Ben that by sharing his love of art with Amelia, he would be helping her to get well again.

Karla was hesitant. "How will Ben get up to the second floor of the home? Do they have an elevator? Is there proper lighting for him to draw and do you think the old lady will have patience with Ben?" She shook her head. "I'm not sure this is a very good idea."

"C'mon Mom! Give me a break, I can do it." Ben turned to his Dad. "How much did you say you would pay?"

Together, father and son dug up the old easel and paints he had used before the accident, last summer. They checked the paint, discarded the old dried up ones, and made a list of the tubes of acrylic colours they would need to have a good supply available. They tested the brushes and included new ones on the growing list. Their arrangement was to go to the art store on Thursday after school to be all ready in preparation for the following Saturday morning. Adam had already confirmed the date with both Amelia and Miss Armstrong.

After Ben had gone to bed, Adam and Karla were having their evening glass of wine together sitting on the couch discussing their days, when Karla put a hand up in apology.

"Oh Adam, I forgot to tell you. Last night when you were at the library, a man called to say he would be coming in to visit you when he returned from Nanaimo. He said he was a flying buddy of yours. He said his name was Jean Paul something. What a gorgeous French Canadian accent he had."

Adam sat back grinning as he thought of his friend Jean Paul, who had been his navigator when they flew reconnaissance over enemy territory in the Middle-East. He recalled all the good, as well as the scary times they had shared. "Well, I'll be darned! It'll be great to see him again."

CHAPTER 9

JEAN PAUL LAVAL FROM QUEBEC, 1954

JEAN PAUL LAVAL WAS A STRONG ATHLETIC FELLOW IN his mid-fifties. He taught environmental studies at McGill University in Montreal during the day, and "worked out" a few nights of the week at the martial arts studio near his apartment. He earned several degrees of black belt, and took part in martial arts tournaments throughout Canada and the USA. When he could afford the time, he also taught the senior classes.

Jean Paul was grieving deeply. His young and beautiful wife had died because of a rapid, unrelenting illness. He felt alone and lost without her.

Making a decision to get away from it all last May, he started out from Montreal, Quebec, riding his Harley motorcycle right across Canada. Many times he had stopped to take in Canada's magnificent vistas as he passed through Ontario, Manitoba, Saskatchewan, and Alberta. He took his time, bunking in some-times with his ex- military buddies or old motorcycle friends. At other times, local people he met and talked with who offered him hospitality since he always appeared to be an affable, relaxed, and an easy going fellow. He made sure he only stayed with couples.

It was close to late autumn in 1954 when he arrived in October 24ᵗʰ This was his final destination: Vancouver Island.

After visiting Victoria's Butchart Gardens and finding a cheap motel, he decided to bike up island to Nanaimo . Jean Paul also wanted to check in with his good friend Adam Wheeler, after he returned.

His friend, Adam had been the pilot of a CH147 Chinook helicopter and Jean Paul was his navigator and paramedic when they flew difficult missions over and into enemy territory. Jean Paul and Adam were fast and true buddies, sticking together through thick and thin.

Adam now lived in Victoria. Two years ago was the last time the two men had seen each other. He kidded Adam about wanting to be a shrink but was pleased he had enrolled in the University of Victoria to study psychology.

Jean Paul grinned, remembering both the many antics as well as the hair raising experiences they had shared. The night before he left, he phoned the Wheeler home and left a message with Adam's wife, Karla. Jean Paul told her he intended to visit them later in the month when he returned to Victoria.

He liked to get up early. He had gassed up his Harley the previous evening and was anxious to set out for Nanaimo before dawn. It was Thursday, October 25 and the early morning air seemed clear, and fresh.

The slight autumn breeze seemed to soften the deep lines in his tanned face as he drove along. Although an excellent and experienced motorcyclist, he was unfamiliar with the Trans-Canada Highway #1 which often has terrible accidents at night or in rainy weather. However on sunny days this route has some spectacular sights of the Pacific Ocean. On a clear day one can stop at some of the lookout places that are situated high above the ocean. From there one sees miles of ocean, different boats meandering among the islands or the peninsula, and more ocean on the other side of another land mass.

The highway's beauty is famous on the island; it is also well known for being winding, narrow and very treacherous, especially at high speeds. The First Nations people named the mountain "Malahat" because the path, which later became the Trans-Canada Highway was very winding like a caterpillar's journey. Malahat means caterpillar.

As he rode along on his motorcycle, Jean Paul's thoughts were of Angela, his deceased wife, and he spoke to the spirit of her memory gently as he remembered her beautiful smile, her musical laugh, and the kindness she shared with everyone in her world.

Sighing, he said, "Ma belle, Angel, why were you taken from me so quickly? We didn't have much time, even to say goodbye. You were so young. God, how I miss you."

Intent on his thoughts, he didn't have time to react quickly when a car burst around a curve in the road above him, weaving from side to side. Travelling at high speed, the car arced across the white line, heading straight for him. Tires squealed when the driver saw him, but it was too late. Jean Paul was side swiped, flung into the air, still on his motorcycle. Over the steep incline they went, banging down, he thrown one way and the bike another.

Now in two separate, tangled masses of underbrush, branches, and earth, they plunged crazily downwards. The bike was deflected several times by trees, so both bike and rider landed close beside a clump of cedar trees in the little valley below.

There seemed to be no one around to help him, or to have witnessed the accident. The sun was rising on that very early autumn morning, and Jean Paul lay sprawled out like a rag doll.

Completely unconscious, with one leg bent terribly out of shape, bleeding profusely, his helmet pulled askew over his face and his arms spread wide open, he seemed almost in a position of supplication to the universe. Above him, the cedar trees moved gently in the early morning breeze, spreading their branches over his inert body, making him almost invisible to the outside world. The crumpled motorcycle beside him coughed, rumbled intermittently, then died. It was the only visual or audible evidence of that brutal accident in the growing light of day.

A startled bird who had nested in the tree above returned to its nest, having recovered from its shock at the accident it had witnessed. It began to chirp weakly.

In the ensuing quiet , the untrained eye would probably have missed the translucent spirit figure of a young woman who drifted gently down beside Jean Paul's body, pushed his helmet back a little, kissed him, and placed her hands first on his bleeding leg and then on his chest in a gesture of healing.

CHAPTER 10

THE RESCUE, OCT. 25, 1954

HANS BURKHART AND CRAIG EMERSON WERE LIFELONG friends ever since they could remember. Their families lived next door to each other, and got along so well that the two groups seemed melded together in harmony as one extended family.

Hans' dad, Adolph, had a very responsible position with the city. He was head of the CRD (Capital Regional District) and could troubleshoot any difficulties within the city. He also maintained a quality control position for Happy Days Retirement Home in Langford. Hans was a student at Victoria College, studying mechanics. Victoria College had united with the Normal School on the Lansdowne campus, which was previously used as a military hospital during World War 2. Hans was blonde, blue eyed, of medium height, with a stocky frame that showed both strength and power. Craig was taller, with dark wavy hair, and slimly built. He looked much more serious than Hans, who made everyone laugh.

Craig was studying medicine in the University of Victoria. His dad was head of the Psychology Department.

Hans owned and rode a Honda motorcycle, and frequently took Craig along as his passenger.

It was Thursday, the 25th of October, promising to be a beautiful sunny autumn day, and they had arranged to take that day off from school and their part time jobs. They set out very early, following a quick breakfast, as dawn was breaking.

As the young men neared the second and most spectacular scenic turn off Hans shouted, "What the hell?" He pointed at the pavement. There were dark, nasty skid marks on the road, before the turn off, and a scraping mark on the little barrier to mark the steep incline on the other side.

He slowed down quickly to a stop.

"Jesus Christ! What happened here?" Craig jumped off the motorcycle even before Hans had stopped the motor. They searched the landscape.

Hans' stomach started to contort in apprehension as he took a step closer to the ridge for a better look.

"Craig! My God! Look!" Hans pointed. "Look over here! It's a Harley!" His breath drew short. Something was terribly wrong. There was a great streak of fresh tracks that gorged and tattered the hillside down to a clump of cedars where a motorcycle was keeled over, parts strewn across the crash.

Turning around and almost pulling Craig off balance, they both took in the eerie sight. Then a faint sound reached them, a raspy weak sound of pain. "Holy smoke! There's someone down there." Craig yelled turning to Hans with a *what do we do* expression. The sound came again, long and groaning but growing fainter. Hans couldn't think; he bolted downwards not calculating the steep drop.

"Hans, *no*! Watch it!"

Hans was airborne for only a second, but panic rose as he hit the steep slope. He rolled sideways to keep balance, dropped on all fours to slow down. His face and arms were searing, but his mind seemed to clear up. "Craig, go get someone! Get an ambulance."

A car had pulled into the area. Craig ran to it, explaining to the driver, "There's been an accident. Some one's been hurt bad down there. Can you get an ambulance or the police, or both?" The driver nodded. "I'll get them here. You go down and take care of whoever's down there."

A now steadier Craig began tediously crawling down the slope, while Hans refocused and cautiously began crawling down the rest of the steep incline, redoubling his efforts to reach the bottom. He ran towards the clump of cedars, shaking now, peering over the bushes and around the cedar trees. He hollered, "Is anyone out here?"

There was movement; he heard the groan and a hand made its slow trembling way from under a cedar tree. Hans rushed to the body; Craig not far behind. The scene shook Hans at first. The man's leg was bent in such a way it was grotesque. Bone protruded from the knee joint, blood oozed from both legs and up to his torso. Hans felt light-headed and dizzy. He thought he was going to faint.

Craig pushed him aside and knelt down beside the injured man

"He's got a pulse, but it's weak." Craig was pale but now calm. He started removing his shirt, facing the man.

"Hey! You're going to make it, man, don't worry, I'm here to help. This will only hurt a second."

Hans stood confused as Craig started tightening the fabric around the man's broken leg.

The bleeding seemed to abate. Craig felt like throwing up, hoped he wouldn't, and kept breathing deeply trying to calm himself.

"Go get the rolled up blanket from your bike, Hans," he commanded in a voice that squeaked at the end of his sentence. *Damn*, he said to himself. *I sound like a girl.*

Craig kept checking the injured man, before carefully removing the helmet from his face. He saw that the man was trying to open his eyes. Soothing him, he repeated, "You'll be all right, man. You're tough. You'll make it!"

The sound of sirens was coming closer. "Help's already on the way."

"Hans, where the hell's that blanket?" He shouted up the slope in a voice more controlled now.

The siren had stopped above them.

"Must be the police as well," he muttered.

The injured man was trying to speak. "Angel, my Angela, where are you?" He opened his eyes again and looked straight at Craig,

"Where did she go?"

"Where did who go?" Craig wondered at the question. "Who is Angela? Can you feel your legs?"

"Yes, my right one is hurting bad! But where is my wife? Where are we? Oh God, what am I doing here under this tree?"

Craig persisted. "Can you move your arms? Can you feel your hands?"

"Yes, yes," Jean Paul muttered, drifting back into unconsciousness.

Craig wondered if they had missed another rider with the injured man, a woman named Angela. He glanced around to see if there was any sign of her.

The sirens close by had stopped. The sound of more sirens kept wailing nearer and nearer through the stillness.

Hans scrambled to the top in time to see a patrol car pull into the viewing area.

"He's down there." He pointed to the right and down. "And he's badly hurt. I don't think he's conscious." The patrol officer was already on his radio device, as Hans went back down the incline with the blanket.

The ambulances soon arrived; the paramedics took over. They placed the man on a stretcher and into the ambulance quickly, reassuring the two boys, and asking them to follow to the Victoria General Hospital.

CHAPTER II

DR. ALLAN GREGORY, OCTOBER 25, 1954

HANS AND CRAIG EAGERLY FOLLOWED THE AMBULANCE back to Victoria in a speedy procession. The doctor in Emergency had an English accent. His name was Dr. Gregory.

"How exactly was he lying? What did you do for him? Did you move him at all?"

Craig answered. "No, we did not move him. I stemmed the blood flow with my shirt. We kept him warm with a blanket. His helmet was still on but across his face a little bit. I gently took it off see whether he would regain consciousness, so I could talk to him. "He was asking about another person; I think her name was Angel or Angela. We saw no evidence of her anywhere, but our man was very concerned. While the paramedics were working, my buddy and I both looked all over the little valley, but there was no trace of anyone else."

The doctor responded. "I'd appreciate it if you would stay until we get our patient stabilized." He disappeared back through the emergency doors.

A few moments later a nurse came out and spoke to the young men. "The man's name is Jean Paul Laval, and his driver's license is from the province of Quebec. You're to wait here."

Soon Dr. Gregory came to talk to the boys again. "He's now awake. He wants to talk to you. Make it fast, fellas, he's going to the OR. By the way, Angel was his late wife. She died a while ago."

Jean Paul was bandaged, and sedated, with intravenous tubes and other tubes going in and out of his body. The part of his skin that was still visible was badly bruised. He was determined to meet the two motorcyclists.

"Thank you for giving me back my life," he said quietly.

The young men were at a loss for words. "We just did what we had to do." Craig gulped.

Hans started to ask about the Harley. The nurse frowned disapprovingly at them. "It's time to go."

As the stretcher moved into the elevator, Jean Paul waved weakly. Hans and Craig heard him call back, "À demain, mes amies." The elevator closed.

Hans spoke up impatiently. "I wanted to tell him I could work on the Harley!"

"Maybe later when he's awake and the operation's a success," Craig said. "Would you believe what has happened today?" The two young men left the building still a little dazed.

• • • • • • •

At about the same time as the young men left the hospital, Otto was in Betty's office explaining to her that he wanted to retire from medicine. They had discussed the changes he had made regarding the board, and Betty had agreed to become the administrator of the home.

She was very fond of Otto and trusted him. He would be 80 in the spring. In confidence, he mentioned to her that he had recently hired a doctor who had arrived from England. The new doctor was to attend to the home's clients and to head the board of directors.

"Hilda and I want to take cruises and travel." He smiled, and in an afterthought said, "Hilda asked me to hire someone else rather than have her head of directors.

"What's his name and when is he coming here?" asked Betty.

The doctor's name is Allan Gregory. The man is smart. He's been a doctor without borders after the last war, lots of experience in running facilities, instrumental in forming clinics for the elderly in Ireland, and now wants a full time position and to settle down."

With a twinkle in his eye, he added, "He's divorced, is a nice looking chap and I think you'll like him."

"I hope you're not thinking of playing cupid doctor." She added, "I've sworn off men, you know."

· · · · · · ·

Allan Gregory sat in the doctor's change room sipping a cup of coffee. He was tired. He had finished his shift very late. There had been numerous accidents during the night shift and before he was ready to leave, there was that motorcycle accident.

"What a bad fracture! Poor guy. Hope he doesn't lose the leg."

The day shift doctor came late, and was apologetic. It didn't lessen the fatigue Dr. Gregory was feeling. He wished he hadn't promised Dr. Burkhart to visit Happy Days Retirement Home, but Dr. Burkhart had hired him as attending physician, and wanted him there immediately.

He made a call to the retirement home and spoke to Betty Armstrong telling her that he would drop in later after he showered and changed at his apartment. Betty said she would be waiting to greet him, and show him around.

He wondered what she would be like. Easy to work with? Or an egotistical bossy nurse who had great expectations? At least she had a lovely low voice on the phone.

Betty was wondering what the new doctor would be like. Bossy? Good or bad bedside manner? He had a British accent, but his was much easier to understand than many she had heard. She liked the timber of his voice and the way he had asked about the clients in the residence. She knew his approximate age; Otto had already told her that. She let her mind slide over other details like, "Is he good looking, tall, intelligent, is he a hot shot or a real honest and compassionate doctor?" Then she gave herself a real shake asking herself, *Betty! Are you lonesome?*

CHAPTER 12

FOLLOWING THE ACCIDENT

IN ANOTHER PART OF TOWN HANS WAS TELLING HIS
father Adolph about the broken down Harley that he wanted to
get permission to use in his mechanics class.

"It would be an awesome project! I could get parts from that
new Harley place going up outside of the mall. I'll need some
added financial help to get it out from the police yard. Hope he'll
sign the consent form. If he does, would you help me, Dad?"

Hans explained he intended to ask Jean Paul's permission. "I'm
not sure if he understood because he was sedated and going to
the OR."

"Hans! Did you get on the poor man's case so soon?"

"I wanted to, but the nurse cut me off."

"Son, you have to be more considerate. The man had a terrible
accident. It will take a while before he gets his bearings again."

"Would you check the consent form? All I need is Jean Paul's
signature and it's a go."

DORIS MAE HONER

Hans and Craig had been in constant connection with the Victoria General's nursing staff, asking for visiting privileges. Jean Paul was now out of Intensive Care and in a private room. He could receive visitors.

Excitedly, Hans and Craig motored up to the Victoria General Hospital, entered the lobby, and asked reception for his room number.

When they entered his room, they were startled to find Jean Paul sitting in bed with his bandaged leg supported and raised halfway up in a frame and weights. His bruised face creased in a big welcoming smile.

"You two are the guys who saved my life!" He held out a big hand grabbing and pulling Craig into a crushing bear hug.

"If it wasn't for you two, I guess I was a gonner." Hans laughed but stood away from those strong muscular arms. He wanted to talk business.

"Hey, you're looking better now. Can't say the same for your bike, though."

"Details, details!" Jean Paul roared still grinning. "What's important is I'm still here. I'll have to find a place to keep what's left of her in a garage."

At that moment Hans' eyes became alight with purpose and he straightened himself up somewhat professionally.

"Well, sir, I've got a plan that could help us both"

"Me, help you?" The big man asked, still grinning widely. "How can I help you? I can't even walk yet."

"Oh no, hold on now, you don't even have to leave your bed." Hans smiled. "How would you like us to fix your bike?" Jean Paul burst out laughing.

"I think I got too much morphine, that, or you guys that just saved my life are trying to save my bike as well. You kids mechanics?"

Hans pulled up a chair and sat down beside the bed.

60

"Think of it as borrowing your bike. I'm studying mechanical engineering, not to brag, but I'm a pretty good mechanic. A piece like that will be real popular at the shop. My bike's a Honda, but someday I'll own a Harley, too."

Jean Paul examined the consent form Hans handed him. "This looks pretty good to me."

Hans gave Jean Paul a book to support the paper, and held out his pen for a signature. "If you sign this paper, my dad will pay the cost of moving her from the police yard to the college. When you're well enough, come see what I've done to get her back in shape again."

Jean Paul took the pen offered to him, read the consent form again, grinned, and signed it with a flourish.

After that, the men spoke of motorcycles, and travels. Hans and Craig plied Jean Paul with questions, until the nurse came with medications and asked the two young men to leave, explaining that her patient was still pretty banged up, and needs more rest.

Before the door had closed, they heard Jean Paul call out, "À demain, mes amies. Come back soon."

. . . .

At the Happy Day's Retirement Home, a long black funeral limousine was parked at the side entrance, waiting to take a deceased body for funeral preparation. The stretcher's destination was to the room next to Amelia's on the second floor.

The resident living there had been ill and bed ridden for many months. She died during the night.

CHAPTER 13

AMELIA, ADAM AND THERAPY, BEGINNING JANUARY 1955

AMELIA GREETED ADAM WHEELER WARMLY THE NEXT morning. She called the kitchen early to order a pot of coffee, asking that it be delivered at 10:30. It arrived a few minutes before Adam tapped on her door. After he was settled, Amelia offered him a cup and poured one for herself. They exchanged pleasantries and then Adam asked, "Tell me about your children. Start with the oldest."

She brought out the family album and showed Adam photos of her sons and daughter. She talked of each one proudly. Adam examined the photos, made comments about who looked like her, and who resembled Adam, then asked kindly, "How did you treat your children?"

She looked surprised at the question. "I was a friend as well as a parent to my children. Are you talking about discipline? Yes, I did spank them when it was necessary, which wasn't often. Generally, I sent them to their rooms to think over their actions, then later we would talk about the reaction to what they had done as well as different ways of going about things."

She indicated one more photo of a home helper, before she closed the album.

"My mother helped me, and I hired a young girl to come when mom was tired. I loved my kids very much, and I know they loved me when they were growing up. The boys were athletic and loved to camp, hunt and fish with their dad. As a family, we made our own fun by reading at night and discussing what we thought of the stories we read. Sometimes it was pretty hilarious." Amelia smiled, remembering.

"How did your children treat you?" He took down notes on Amelia's attitudes towards children.

As she thought about how the three kids had come to help her, Amelia began to see that the children were very concerned about her and wanted only the best for her. She began to abandon her ideas that no one cared about her.

When Adam began to discuss the various family problems that occurred, he noted that Amelia was becoming much more realistic in her perceptions not only of her family but also her own behaviour. She even admitted that depression had clouded much of her outlook.

Adam told her a little of his own family, especially centering on Ben, since Amelia had asked about him as far as teaching him the basics of art and composition. He still delivered papers with the help of his mother, Karla.

Then Adam looked at his watch. "I'd like to find out about your work history. Are you tired? May I come back next week, on Thursday at 10:30?"

"Of course," Amelia replied. "We'll talk about the old days."

She walked Adam to the door, smiled, and then shook his hand warmly.

When she returned to her easy chair, she sat in silence for a long time thinking about their conversation. All day Amelia was both restless and thoughtful. After supper, she sat in her room fiddling with a bit of crochet. She stayed up way past her bedtime, thinking.

Adam seems to have made me see things in a whole new light. What am I doing to help myself?

Am I angry at my own kids for moving away and putting me here, and at Adam and my favourite uncle, as well as my mother for dying on me? She put on her nightie, reached for the lamp, turned it off, and tucked herself into bed to sleep.

The following Thursday morning saw Amelia up and ready for the interview. As Adam sat down, she offered him a cup of coffee and said, "There's not much more to tell you about me. I went to high school and took many commercial subjects. When I finished high school, I got married right away, even when mom wanted me to go to university."

"Did you and your mom butt heads often?"

"Yes, my mom often said she hoped I would grow up and have a little girl like me."

"Do you think your mom loved you?"

Amelia's answer came softly. "Yes, I know now she loved me very much. We had a wonderful relationship in my adult years and she always supported me and never let me down. I miss her now she's gone." Amelia looked sad, then brightened. "She said we were made from the wood of the same tree, somewhat stubborn and impatient, don't you think?"

"What other kind of work did you do?"

"When Adam and I had the farm, I did farm chores, and helped him with his work, too. I was strong in those days. Once the kids came, I helped them, sang to them, and taught them as much about school as I could. We were so far away from town that I home schooled them. When we moved into town, they went to a real school and I went to work in an office, first an accountant's office, and later I worked for a lawyer."

"How did you get along as a secretary?"

"I think I did pretty well. They always gave me annual raises, and a nice bonus at Christmas, too. The accountant was sorry to see me go, but I was getting bored there, so when Mr. Dawson, the lawyer, needed someone, I applied and got the job."

"How was it for you working with lawyers?"

"Actually, I surprised everyone because I caught on real fast and studied at night school. I wanted to do a good job. I did well too. The work was much more interesting and I liked dealing with the people."

"When your children grew up and left the nest, what did you do then?"

Amelia paused, looked down at her hands, and sighed deeply.

"Soon after they left, Adam had that awful accident. Two of the boys tried to help, but they wanted to keep the jobs they had found in northern Alberta. Of course, my daughter couldn't come because her husband was posted in Alaska."

"I want to hear more about Adam, and the accident. But right now I have to catch my next class."

Adam rose, grabbed his windbreaker, gave Amelia a wide grin, and asked as he loped towards the door. "Next Thursday at 10:30 okay for you?"

"Agreed." Amelia smiled and he was gone.

CHAPTER 14

PAINFUL THERAPY AND BREAKTHROUGH.

ADAM BEGAN TO ENJOY GREATLY HIS SESSIONS WITH Amelia. He believed that Amelia opened up to him more readily because his name was Adam and he reminded her of her late husband Adam Archer. Today, they had chatted about how well she was feeling lately, how Adam was doing in school, and the weather. Now Adam was ready to ask Amelia specific questions, which he knew would be difficult for her to answer.

His notebook was open and ready. He looked directly at Amelia with a kind, fond expression on his face.

"What exactly happened to your husband, Adam Archer, Amelia? I want you to tell me all you remember about the accident."

Amelia's facial expression turned from relaxed and pleasant to one of deep painful sadness. Slowly, with reluctance, she began.

"My husband was working on the railway. It was winter and during a bad storm. He was trying to release one of the actions on the rail that had jammed. He and his assistant both had earplugs on because they were using snow blowers to clear the rails. Neither of them heard the train coming. It was unscheduled and a late arrival because of the storm. What, with the wind howling like it was when his assistant saw the lights of the train, he jumped out of the way, pulling Adam behind him as he went. But the train hit Adam sideways. It didn't run over him but sent him flying through the air."

Amelia's voice began to quaver. "When he landed, he was still alive, but his leg and arm were both broken by the fall and he hit his head hard. He must have lost a lot of blood. They phoned me to come to the hospital." She paused and blew her nose in a tissue Adam handed her.

"When I saw him, I barely recognized him. He had tubes coming out of him, and his head was all bandaged up. I couldn't see his face and his eyes were swollen shut. They said his right arm and leg were broken. They were going to operate on him, and put him back together."

She began to tear up again.

Adam shook his head and reached out to her. "That was sure hard to go through, Amelia. Do you wish to go on?"

She nodded her head. "I've never told anyone about this. I need to open it up, Adam." She cleared her throat.

"It was awful, waiting, not knowing. They brought him out of the operating room and into Intensive Care. They told me to go home, but I waited there because I wanted him to know I was there when he woke up." As the painful memories came flooding back, she began to weep, and covered her mouth with her hanky, which she grasped with both hands. It took her a while to regain control, as Adam waited very quietly. He got up and made them both a cup of coffee. She nodded "thank you." Then she went on.

"His bones healed, but his spine was damaged from the fall and he could never walk again. He couldn't do much after that." She sighed. "And he wasn't right in his head." Adam brought his chair over to where Amelia was sitting and placed it right beside her.

He put one big hand over her little one and patted it gently. She leaned back, and took a deep breath.

"I've never talked to anyone about all those details of the accident. It's brought it all right back, but I'm glad I told you." She sipped her coffee. "Besides Adam's bad back injury, the doctor said that some of his organs were damaged. Adam came home after his stay in hospital and I took care of him." Amelia looked tired.

"He couldn't do anything for himself. I took care of him night and day, for almost two years, and he began to re-learn some things, but then he had a major stroke and he died."

"Wow! You took care of him for such a long time! That must have been hard. Wasn't there anyone to help you?" Adam's face was full of sympathy. He put an arm around her shoulders and she leaned on him, then straightened up.

"Adam, it was very, very hard. My husband was a good man and he suffered a lot. So did I. The worst part of it was, I seemed to be taking care of someone I didn't know. I had to feed him, change his diapers, make sure his skin didn't break down from all that lying in bed, and there wasn't anyone to help me or talk to me. Once in a while the doctor came by and once he brought a nurse to give me a break. The ladies at the church helped me some, staying with him while I shopped for groceries or even to have an undisturbed sleep."

"What about your children, Amelia? Didn't they help?"

She answered slowly. "That was another problem. I was angry at them all for not coming. But they had all gone: two in Alberta, one in Manitoba, and my daughter had married an American pilot and was up in Alaska. The two in Alberta were isolated; the one in Manitoba was stuck in his new job, and my daughter had suffered a miscarriage."

Amelia began to rock herself back and forth as she held her hands folded under her chest. Her head was bent and she looked like a sad little child. Adam caught her by her shoulders and gently brought her back from her memories.

"Amelia, you are here *now*. What you are telling me happened in the past." Then he asked her if she wanted more coffee.

They chatted a bit about the weather; it had stopped raining and the sun was peeking out. She turned to him. "Adam, I must get all of this out in the open." She took another sip of coffee and then grimly resumed.

"It seemed like there was never going to be an end to it. I am ashamed to admit this, and I've never confessed this to anyone. But sometimes I wished that he would die. I needed relief from it all." This time she blew her nose, gave a great big sigh, and smiled quaveringly at him.

Adam quietly nodded. "I can understand those thoughts. They are very normal, under those conditions." He waited for her to continue.

She shook her head from side to side, but her voice was stronger, as if she was now aware this was the present, and all she had been through was now in the past. "There was no way he could get better and be the man I was married to."

Adam spoke softly in a deeply compassionate voice. "Amelia, that was a real hard load for you to carry, and for two years! Anyone would wish themselves out of it under those circumstances. You mustn't blame yourself. You did the very best you could for such a long time and under miserable conditions. How do you feel right now?"

She had stopped crying and the light of energy was coming back into her eyes. "I put a tremendous burden down somewhere. It's like the sun is coming out again." She laughed weakly and pointed to the window, where the sun was beginning to peek out from the clouds.

"You did an amazing job, and for so long Amelia. I'm sure you helped your Adam far more than you will ever know." Adam got up and put the coffee cups in the sink. "Were your children able to come to Adam's funeral?"

"After Adam died, two of my boys came back briefly but were in a hurry to return to their camps since they were on the right track, they said, to discovering oil."

"What about Sarah, your daughter?" Adam asked.

"She was at the end of another pregnancy and the doctor didn't want her to travel. My middle son, John, was still working as well as in university and it was exam time."

"What happened then, Amelia?" Adam asked gently, returning to his open notebook on the desk.

"Well, my mother kept writing, suggesting I move close to her in Victoria, BC where she was enjoying life and visiting often with her brother. He was my favourite uncle. After the funeral I did just that. I packed up some of my things, put them in a truck, then sold the farm. Can you believe it? I drove right through Saskatchewan, Alberta and into BC in my truck, and got to Victoria in one piece. I found an apartment and settled in." She smiled at the memory of her travels and adventures.

"Did you start work again?"

"No. I thought I needed time to get accustomed to my new surroundings. Victoria is not a bit like Saskatchewan, and I didn't feel like working. I had some money from the sale of the farm, and I thought I would take some time off. But as time went on I began to lose energy and grieve more. My uncle took me to his doctor and they started putting me on some pills. Anti-depressants, they said."

"Did the pills help?"

She shook her head. "Maybe they did and maybe they didn't. The doctor was busy; he didn't see me often and I didn't like him, anyway. My mom and uncle tried to help me, but he had cancer. Then out of the blue my mom had a massive stroke and died right there on the spot! Uncle Tommy followed her about a month after that."

Adam's face was full of compassion and sympathy. "That must have been hard when you were coming up from your grief."

"Yes." It was too much for me I guess. I hadn't made any friends yet, any good ones I mean. And I felt all alone. I have a sister-in-law up in Nanaimo. We were very close as children and she's Adam's sister. She came to see me after uncle died and brought my family here to help me. I was mad at her for interfering, but I guess I was in bad shape."

Adam was scribbling notes in his book, looked up and smiled.

"What makes you say that, Amelia? You said I guess I was in bad shape?"

"When my sons came to visit, they were real surprised at the change in me. None of them wanted to take me to their cabins in northern Alberta. I don't blame them; there are no facilities there, and I didn't want that, either. My daughter flew in from Alaska and brought my grandchild. She agreed with the boys that I needed help. So here I am."

Adam grinned a little grin. "What do you think now, Amelia?"

"Well, that's what is interesting. When I started here, all I wanted to do was die off quickly. Old Dr. Burkhart said I had Alzheimer's disease and put me on more pills. I didn't care and wished he'd give me enough to put me out. I almost enjoyed acting the part by giving him stupid answers when he came to see me. But that head nurse, she knew better, and I didn't fool her one bit. But I wanted to get life over with."

"You were taking a lot of pills? Are you still on them?"

"Not any more. I started cutting back on them, by just holding some in my mouth till the nurse left, then I'd spit those out in the toilet and flush it. Funny, after that my head started to clear."

"Are you still cutting down in the pills or have you stopped them?"

I take the white one in the morning and at night time. I think that one helps me because I'm more calm. The rest of them I get rid of."

"Have you seen the new doctor yet?"

"No, I haven't and if he gets mad at me for non-compliance, I am not going to worry about it."

"You've been through a great deal of trial, more than enough to knock anyone off their feet. But you seem to be coming out of it. What do you think?"

"I know talking to you has really helped me. Lori, our nurse's aide, has kept me more upbeat with all her chatting and warmth. Today I've been able to go into that deep dark place and tell you about it. Honestly, that part of my life is now done. One thing I do know; that awful gnawing pain has lessened inside of me." She looked at Adam with real affection.

"You know the one I mean," she considered. "It isn't physical; it's a heavy aching painful feeling inside that doesn't go away. It's a pain in the soul." She smiled. "It's good to have trusted people to talk to. Everyone needs someone to trust and talk to."

Adam considered for a moment, smiled slightly, and asked, "Depression involves anger as well as pain internalized. You were justified to feel angry, abandoned, and alone. You were that in your own mind. Do you think if you had made a trusted friend you would have had a chance to help yourself?" She nodded her head.

"But now you look like you're coming up and seeing things in a brighter light."

She nodded her head again.

"On our next session," Adam suggested, "let's talk about your present skills and the upcoming art lessons with Ben." He checked his watch.

"Holy jumpin' Jupiter! I've missed half my next lecture. "Amelia, I have to run! Grabbing his coat, he asked, "Next Thursday at 10:30? We'll plan the art lessons with Ben, okay?"

CHAPTER 15

SATURDAY MORNING WITH BEN

I WAS BEGINNING TO READ THE NANAIMO EVENING PAPER and having a nice cup of coffee Saturday night when Amelia phoned me. I had sat down right after I'd done the supper dishes and was ready to relax.

Amelia was all excited and was itching to tell me something. She said she had met Adam's son, Ben, and he was sooo cute! She was so excited, her words got all garbled at times.

"Slow down, Amelia" I had to say to her, several times.

I'll try to repeat it, since her experience with Ben was such a surprise.

"It was about 10:20 in the morning and I heard this sharp tapping on my door. Adam had explained on Friday that Ben wanted to meet me by himself. He said that Ben had told him to be at the door downstairs for 11:30, but that he wished to go up to my room by himself. Apparently, he was tickled because he regarded the art meeting as his first real job.

"I opened the door looking straight ahead, and this hoarse little voice said, "I'm down here!" When I looked down, there he was, sitting straight in his wheel chair. He held out his hand. "I am Ben, Adam's son. I believe you are Amelia. Is it okay if I call you "Amelia?" That would make me feel better, since I'm here to teach you how to sketch. I hate having to be formal if you are going to be my student.'"

Then he reached up again to shake my hand. Amelia giggled.

"I looked into his big brown eyes, in a little round face with a few freckles spread across his nose and onto his cheeks. His brown hair was as curly as his dad's. Then Ben smiled with one tooth missing. Honestly, Margaret," Amelia said, "I melted right on the spot."

He had a large sketch- book on his lap, and a bag carrying his crayons or charcoal beside it.

After we shook hands, I stood aside and gestured for him to come into my room. I had set it up for the art lesson, and asked Ben if he needed help taking off his jacket.

"No, thank you, I manage a lot by myself." He wiggled out of it. "Where will I put this?"

I took it from him and hung it in the closet beside the door.

"Dad told me you're quite a painter. Can I see what you've done? Dad said your pictures are really good. I'd like to see them."

Margaret, I swear that this kid is eight going on 28. I showed him the paintings hanging on the wall and Ben scrutinized each one carefully. When he was done he said, "Well, you certainly have a lot of talent in water colours and acrylics. I'd call you a first rate landscape artist. Do you want to see what I've done?" He opened his sketch- book and I was amazed at what he showed me. There were sketches of his dad, Adam, and his mother, Karla, as well as several of his dog, Scruffy. The sketches were anything but childlike. They were as sure and certain as what any skilled portrait artist would do.

I said, "I've never done charcoal." Then innocently I asked, "Did anyone help you with these sketches, Ben?"

His face clouded a bit and he regarded me silently, before he said, "Please, I know I'm good. Everyone says so at school. But yes, I do have an art teacher who is a friend of Dad's. He taught me how to organize my eyes. Now let's get on with your lesson. I'd like to teach you how to use charcoal and sketch. Do you know anything about using charcoal?"

"No, I don't. And I don't have a sketch book."

"That's okay. I brought one. It's in the big pocket on the other side of my back support." He indicated by pointing over his shoulder towards his back. I went and took it out of the pocket. He spread some charcoal out on a piece of cloth, and explained how to hold the piece of charcoal and not to press too hard.

We agreed that I could sketch Ben and he would check my work and then we could discuss it together.

Amelia was laughing so hard on the phone; she could hardly talk.

"The thing is, I have never used charcoal before and needed his instruction not only on using it, but also doing portraits, since I'm a landscape artist. My sketch of Ben was pretty tragic." Amelia went into another fit of laughter.

I waited for her to catch her breath. "Then what happened?"

"Ben gave me my first lesson on how to 'organize my eyes'. He told me to look at his face and divide it into four parts. Then he said to carefully put everything where it belonged in each of the four parts. He added that no two sections of a face were exactly alike, that there were very slight variations that the onlooker wouldn't even recognize, unless they knew how to 'organize their eyes.' When we had finished the charcoal lesson, Ben looked at my sketch and gave me some real emotional support. He said I would improve by 'doing', and reassured me that he knew I would be good at sketching because he had a 'feeling' about it. Then he said, 'I know nothing about landscape art yet. Maybe you might teach me how to paint?'

Amelia's voice became very serious, and with real respect she described the rest of the discussion and the upcoming next lesson with Ben where after he had posed for her to sketch him again, she would teach him about water colours and landscape painting.

"I hope I can be as organized as Ben. I think he is a very mature adult in a little boy's body. He is such an amazing little fellow. He never lost his concentration. He's a real intelligent kid. He's incredible."

I could tell from her previous laughter and now the tenderness and emotion in her voice that Amelia's art lesson had gone far better than anyone could have imagined.

CHAPTER 16

RENEWAL

"MARGARET! YOU'LL NEVER GUESS WHAT HAPPENED YES-terday!" It was Amelia, at 7:30 on Saturday morning, my day off work. She began keeping me informed by phone ever since young Ben had begun teaching her to do portrait sketches. I learned that Ben was doing well learning landscape painting and Amelia was managing to make her sketches of Ben look like him. Apparently they both laughed together more and more, and I knew right then that Amelia was returning to the Amelia I knew, my long- time friend and also my sister-in-law.

Betty Armstrong usually phoned around 9:00 am. She also kept me up to date regarding Amelia and the new Dr. Allan Gregory, who had become the chief physician. I suspect Betty was more than casually interested in the new doctor, but she would be the last to admit it.

The fact that Dr. Burkhart had put the retirement home up for sale, then took it off the market, did interest me, and I hadn't been given any more news about that recently. Betty said she had made an offer on it, and Dr. Gregory had made one also.

Betty told me Dr. Gregory had been working very long hours in Victoria General, and was getting tired. He was coming to the end of working in the Emergency Department. He loved working with the aging population, and when Dr. Burkhart mentioned to him that he was putting the Happy Days Retirement Home up for sale, Dr. Gregory quickly contacted both the state company regarding the building, and the Health Care Representative concerning the resident population, and put in offers. He was greatly surprised when both representatives had phoned, letting him know that the retirement home had been taken off the market.

He was new to the region, having immigrated into Canada from England. He and his wife had divorced; his children were grown and on their own now, and he wanted a new start in a new land. His qualifications were quite impressive; he was a specialist in internal medicine, was consulted regularly regarding his specialty in the study of the aging populations, and he had been sought after to establish a practice in Ireland specializing in the health and welfare of the maturing adult. He had enjoyed setting up this particular practice, and trained others to take his place before immigrating to Canada. He noticed that the Happy Days Retirement Home was reputed to be a facility for the poor.

When he visited the home, he observed the resident's meals were sparse, the activity program was almost non- existent, and people were always breaking limbs from falls. There was an RN in charge, but most of the staff appeared to be untrained attendants. He saw many areas that needed improvement in the shabby facility, but since he was about to start there as Chief Physician he had not begun to ask questions of the administration, and was observing closely what was going on there.

He easily slung his long frame into a comfortable chair in his rented apartment, and sipped thoughtfully on a glass of wine.

I'll need to have a closer look at the Canadian provincial laws for the protection of clients in retirement homes. Tomorrow, I'd better take time to read the literature I was given by one of the doctors I'm helping in Emergency.

His thoughts wandered back to the retirement home and about what the RN had told him about a client who had cut out her many medications, antidepressants as well as the many prescriptions for people with Alzheimer's disease. That interested him since she had done it on her own without permission from Dr. Burkhart.

· · · · · · ·

The next day, late in the afternoon, Betty tapped on Amelia's door, before entering.

Betty was amazed when Amelia opened her door and smiled. She couldn't remember whether Amelia had ever smiled before.

"Dr. Gregory will be in to see you in a few days. He wants to check you over and discuss your medications with you."

"Good. I want to talk to him about several things. And while I'm at it, I'd like to ask you a few questions. Will you come in for a chat?" Amelia stood aside and gestured for her to pass.

"Would you like to sit in the easy chair? It's the most comfortable."

Betty sat down, astounded at the change in Amelia. Although Amelia's clothes hung limply on her body from the recent weight loss, she looked more energetic, and youthful.

Why, she's almost attractive. I hadn't noticed that before. Those art lessons with Adam's son Ben must be brightening her up

"I want to go shopping and get some clothes that fit me," Amelia said pulling her clothes out to show how too large they were, hanging limply on her slim frame. "However, I am careful with my money. I used to shop in thrift shops, because I liked the people who worked there and could always find a bargain that fit me just right."

"Shopping is something I can arrange right away," said Betty, "Would you like to go shopping with me? I'm off on Saturday, and could pick you up. I also need some new clothes and know just the place where the clothes are reasonable, in fashion, and usually quite attractive. I shop there all the time when I need something. It's a gently used clothing store off Goldstream Avenue here in Langford, and I think you might like it. If you don't, I'll take you somewhere else. There's a good Salvation Army outlet not too far away."

"That sounds interesting," Amelia responded. "I also want to go to the town library and get some books. I used to love to read." They agreed on a time.

As Betty descended the stairs after seeing Amelia, she wondered what was going on with the retirement home and why it had been taken off the real estate market.

Saturday morning brought sun and blue skies. Betty picked Amelia up at 10:30 sharp and they headed straight for the thrift Store.

"I want a new blouse, and a skirt that fits me. Maybe a pair of shoes as well as sandals or summer shoes of some kind," stated Amelia. "Even my feet seem to have shrunk."

"Sounds good for starters," chuckled Betty.

Together they perused the new thrift store while the staff brought out different skirts and blouses for them to consider. Everyone seemed in such good humour, and there were many happy compliments and giggling as they chose the items they wanted. They returned to Happy Days Retirement in great spirits and Amelia couldn't wait to try on her new clothes again once she reached her room.

On the following Monday morning, Dr. Gregory sat down in the office with Betty, and they discussed Amelia's case history and the present change in Amelia.

"She has brightened up! The major changes began to happen when Adam Wheeler, a psychology student from UVic began visiting her. His notes are in the back of the chart. Now she is giving and receiving art lessons with Adam's son Ben, a very mature 8-year-old and quite an artist. He and Amelia are getting on famously and she's a completely different woman these days."

She rose, gesturing for Dr. Gregory to follow. "I think Amelia's on the mend. Right now, I want you to meet her."

Amelia had been waiting it seemed like hours for the doctor to come. She had washed and dressed herself carefully, put on a light colour of lipstick, blush, eye shadow and eyebrow pencil. She tidied her room several times, went to the cracked mirror that had been screwed onto her door, and smoothed her hair once more, straightening her brand new skirt and blouse for the ump-teenth time.

The firm knock on the door startled her, then she smiled as she opened it.

"Good morning, Amelia, I'm Dr. Gregory. You asked to see me?" He smiled at Amelia as she looked up at his six-foot frame from her less than five-foot stature. She stood aside and gestured for him to come in and sit down, pointing towards the easy chair.

"Yes. Please come in." She followed him and sat down on the side of her bed. Looking directly at him she said, "I want you to know that I took myself off all the medicines except one that Dr. Burkhart had put me on. I want to live a lot longer now that I have something to live for."

"Oh? Tell me more." After Amelia described her recent art lessons and the change in her feelings, Dr. Gregory asked Amelia about her medications and mentioned that he knew she had been cutting out most of them out.

They discussed the pros and cons of stopping medications without letting the doctor know, then Dr. Gregory said, "All right, Amelia. You are looking pretty well balanced to me. How about if

I prescribe Vitamin B 12, and a few other vitamins that will help pep you up a bit more?"

"What a great idea, Dr. Gregory! Wish I'd thought of it, myself."

CHAPTER 17

KARLA, BETTY AND RESUSCITATION

ADAM WHEELER'S WIFE KARLA, WAS AN ASSISTANT TO A doctor of kinesiology, before receiving her MA, majoring in kinesiology and rehabilitation. After coming to Victoria, she worked in a facility that helped injured clients to regain ambulation in walking, running, and resuming their activities of daily living. She knew a fair amount about rehabilitation, or people in the sports world, was self- employed, and did contract work for various doctors, and agencies.

Karla intended to visit Happy Days Retirement Home and check out how Amelia and Ben were doing with art lessons. She made an appointment with Betty Armstrong and on her day off from work she arrived at the facility early in the morning.

Betty was in her office, and Karla was ushered in to see her by the young secretary. She introduced herself. "My name is Karla Wheeler, I'm Adam's wife. I've come to see how my son's client, Amelia, is doing with her art lessons."

"My specialty is rehabilitation. I work as a consultant in the Jubilee hospital rehabilitation unit, and I am very familiar with hospital protocol."

"My son is very young, only 8-years-old, and wheelchair-bound at present. He was hit by a car, driven by a drunk driver, and suffered a severe spinal injury." She gestured with her hands. "I'm afraid this facility is less than what I expected for a retirement home. Since Ben is wheelchair bound, I want to make sure that he gets to and from his meetings with Amelia safely."

Betty listened intently. She was touched by Karla's sincerity and her knowledge of how the facility was lacking in many ways. Betty was very impressed with Karla, and said so.

"I agree with your assessment of Happy Days Retirement Home. There are improvements coming. I have made sure that your son is given the utmost help in every way that you ask. We have an elevator. Let's go right up. Amelia has made amazing progress since your husband visits her, and now she and Ben are getting on famously. Amelia is an amazing woman. Her transformation is absolutely miraculous."

Karla smiled in appreciation.

Amelia was working on an oil painting of Ben when Betty and Karla tapped on her door. When Karla saw the painting, she stopped and gasped in appreciation.

"Wow! That's really good!"

Amelia smiled broadly. "Do you know this little wizard?"

Karla responded still in amazement. "Why, yes I do. He's my son, and I hope you'll sell this painting to me."

Betty touched Amelia's shoulder. "Amelia, this is Karla Wheeler, who came to see how you and Ben are doing."

She explained that Karla had some concerns about Ben's safety and that since she was Ben's mom she wanted to get to know Amelia.

"My son is so young and such a bright little fellow."

Amelia's eyes widened as she listened to Karla's worries. When Karla had finished talking, Amelia reassured her. "Ben is an amazing little man. I always make sure he gets safely to the front door where his dad waits for him. We always take the elevator down, then I walk along with him to meet his dad and we chat mostly about art techniques while we come down. Despite being wheelchair bound, he and I have arranged that we teach each other. We are exploring the art world together. Ben is really bright."

In the parking lot below, a black BMW pulled into the space marked "Doctor." Dr. Burkhart had come to say a goodbye to the Happy Days Residence he loved, before he and his wife went on a cruise. He was a large worried-looking, white–haired gentleman. He thought to himself that he was feeling a little off his usual self. He was becoming very concerned regarding the financial situation there which was regarding his oldest son.

This was upsetting the elderly doctor greatly. Originally, he had put the home up for sale, along with the patient care for the population in the home. Initially he hoped to leave more money to his children and his grandson. However, after he learned about the mismanagement of both the state of the books, and the home's general deteriorating condition, he had put much concern into how to alter the situation. He and his wife had contacted their lawyer, and made a new will.

Certainly he understood the directives of his sons regarding the home. He blamed himself for establishing them as the board of directors. He knew they wished to keep all expenses down and he disagreed with what it was doing to the clients and the home.

The sons had assumed he would be leaving everything to them. Now that he had observed how the accounts and money were being mismanaged, the final decision regarding the home that he and his wife had drawn up greatly pleased him.

Now he was going to his beloved home to say goodbye and to give that smart RN a bonus cheque and a letter for all her good work and her many wonderful ideas for improving the home. He rubbed at the growing pain in his left arm.

Must have overdone it in golf yesterday. he mused. *Must have pulled a muscle in my back, too. My arm's has been sore all morning.* Slowly, he walked up to the entrance of his building.

Opening the door, a sharp twinge in his chest caught him, and he paused to get his breath back. Walking slowly to the reception desk, he gasped, took an envelope from his vest pocket, said to the receptionist, "Give this to Betty", and fell in a heap at her feet.

The stunned receptionist, who had risen to greet him shouted to the stenographer, "Get an ambulance, and call for Betty!" She kneeled to take his pulse. He was frothing a little at the mouth and all colour had drained from his face. "Get Betty here, stat" she ordered again.

"She's with Amelia Archer, room 24."

Lori, the nurse's aide had stopped in her tracks. Jolting into action, she ran to the stairs and up, two at a time. At the top, she pounded on Amelia's door the same instant that an intercom buzzer rang in Amelia's room.

"Miss Armstrong, quick! Something has happened to Dr. Burkhart. Come quick, come quick!" She cried.

Betty and Karla both raced out of the room, down the stairs and forward to where Dr. Burkhart lay.

"He's still breathing, I think," said the receptionist. Betty checked his chest with her stethoscope. Did she hear something or was it her imagination? Karla listened for breath sounds. She whipped out her compact and stuck it under his nose. A faint clouding there.

"Let's do it," she said and the two women began CPR. Karla asked the receptionist, "Have you called for help?"

"Yes, the ambulance is coming.

In perfect teamwork, Karla and Betty worked on Dr. Burkhart's very still body, with Betty giving CPR, while Karla applied mouth to mouth respiration. A distant ambulance siren wailed closer as they tried desperately to revive him.

The paramedics arrived quickly, took over with oxygen and resuscitation equipment and Dr. Burkhart was quickly transported to the Victoria General Hospital, where Dr. Gregory was waiting to meet them. He and the emergency team worked tirelessly on Dr. Burkhart's inert body. The monitor showed Otto Burkhart's heart began to beat in more steady sinus rhythm. His eyelids fluttered open.

After coughing, he reached up and pulled the oxygen mask off. "What the hell am I doing lying here?" He coughed a bit more. "And why are you all here?" He smiled faintly, put the oxygen mask back on and began to understand. When he opened his eyes once more, he pulled off the mask again, and asked, Are we having a party?" He put the mask back on and began sleeping.

Welcome back" said the relieved Dr. Gregory, patting the old doctor's shoulder. "Now stay with us!" The whole Emergency team gasped happily in great relief.

Otto Burkhart was beloved by all in the hospital.

CHAPTER 18

THE LATEST NEWS

It's time I got a job. Amelia thought to herself. My life isn't over because I've lost the folks I loved. They're gone, but I'm still here and I'm still plenty alive.

She dressed herself quietly, made her bed, tidied her room and sat down at her desk to make a list of things she wanted to get done.

Hmm, first, I had better get some working clothes. Then write to my last boss and ask him to give me a reference if necessary.

It was 3 o'clock in the morning. She had awakened and couldn't get back to sleep. By 5 o'clock she had written her former boss, put the letter in an envelope, addressed, sealed and stamped it, made her shopping list, had a shower, put on some makeup and was dressed ready for the day.

Last night when she returned to her room, she noticed a great change in the bathroom she used, which was also shared with the bedroom on the other side of the bathroom. Previously, she was the only resident using the bathroom, but it appeared now that this situation had changed.

It looked like a man's shaving gear was on one sink, and towels that smelled of shaving lotion were hung next to that sink. Nothing of hers had been touched.

"*Well.*" Amelia locked the door of the room next to hers before stepping into the shower. Looks like there's a man living next door. That should be interesting

Everything was quiet in the next room. She managed to shower and clean the shower stall as quietly as she could, before returning to her room and getting dressed.

The residence was still quiet; most of the people still in bed. She pulled out the book she had taken from the library, and read until she knew the kitchen had opened and was serving breakfast.

I like getting things done early, so I can enjoy the day, she thought as she walked down the stairs to breakfast.

"Why not take the elevator?" The lady across the hall commented as Amelia passed, preparing to take the stairs. Amelia stopped and smiled at the brown, wrinkled face in front of her. Gently she responded, "I'm trying to generate strength by 'doing', I guess."

The more I do then the more I can do, she said to herself, descending the stairs to the dining room.

The home's large dining room has several round wooden tables, with four cushioned wooden chairs around each table. While the residents eat, they socialize and get to know each other in little groups.

Sitting at Amelia's table were three white haired ladies, Jane, a retired teacher from Nanaimo, Marie from the Maritimes, who had been a stenographer and Sarah from Saskatchewan, who had always been a farmer's wife, a mom, and a grandma. The three ladies had become quite fond of Amelia, regarding her as "the new kid" at their table. Jane and Marie were in their seventies and Sara celebrated her 85 birthday.

They were already seated and were giggling and kidding each other when Amelia sat down. "Hey, what's all the excitement about?"

"Haven't you heard?" Jane asked, incredulous that Amelia didn't know what had happened in the facility.

"No," said Amelia. "Why don't you let me in on the joke?"

"He's no joke, Amelia," chortled Marie. "He's good-looking and he's been put in the room next to you! You will both share the same bathroom! WOOWEEEEEEE! Lucky you!"

Amelia looked puzzled. "Ladies, I don't know what you're talking about. I was away most of yesterday. I must have missed everything. Start from the beginning."

"Amelia, we've had a new resident come in." Jane stirred her porridge excitedly.

Marie added, twinkling, "He's a darling man with big muscles."

Sara chimed in, "He had a motorcycle accident about a month ago and broke his leg real bad. He has other cuts and bruises, too, but most are going away now. Dr. Gregory transferred him from the Vic General to recuperate here."

Marie blurted, "He's absolutely gorgeous, Amelia, and has a real cute French accent. He should be coming down soon because he gets up early. He's still in a wheelchair, but he wheels himself around."

"He looks like he's about your age, Amelia." Sara winked and poked Marie in the ribs.

"Amelia, you simply must fill us in when you get to know him." twittered Sarah again, giggling as she spooned in her porridge.

"Guess I was up and away before he got up," Amelia confessed.

She told the girls all about Ben and the portrait she was painting of him. They listened politely, but as soon as she was finished, they kept up about the newcomer, almost in a chorus, "You must tell us all about the new fella, Amelia, when you meet him. He's what we really want to know about."

Amelia shrugged her shoulders, finished her breakfast, smiled and blushed as the ladies pressed her for any details. Then she excused herself politely from the table.

When she got back to her room, she left the door open to hear the elevator door open and shut. She told herself she was expecting Ben and liked to greet him, but her mind wandered to the new man in the room next to hers.

The girls said he was good looking, she mused. *And they said he's my age.*

She peeked out the door through the slit she had opened. *I wonder how I'm going to meet him?*

Then she closed the door and shook herself sharply. *Amelia! Stop being silly,* she commanded to herself.

CHAPTER 19

ANOTHER ART LESSON

AT 9:30 ON A SATURDAY MORNING, AMELIA WAS WAITING for Ben to come for their regular art session. She heard the sound of the elevator coming up, opened her door and walked out to meet him.

When the elevator door opened, she was surprised to see the diminutive, chuckling, smiling Ben talking with animation to a tall, middle-aged, good looking man using crutches.

Ben was beaming radiantly. Turning his head to Amelia, he said, "I brang my friend to meet you, Amelia. He and Dad know each other from the war. Can he come in? He wants to see what I'm doing."

Amelia had been standing in front of the elevator, barring the two from getting out. She wondered if her mouth was gaping open, and quickly moved to receive the two, pointing to her open door. "Please, both of you, go on in." She noticed her voice sounded raspy. The two entered her little apartment, still in lively conversation.

"His name's Jean Paul, Amelia." Ben pointed at the new visitor. "He and Dad were flying buddies." Then, pointing at Amelia and looking towards Jean Paul, he said, "Her name's Amelia. We do art together. She's very good at painting."

Amelia and Jean Paul smiled at each other. Amelia murmured, "Pleased to meet you, Jean Paul."

The big man hobbled over, and took her hand. "Enchanté, madam," he said in a deep melodious voice.

Ben grinned at the two of them, then saw Amelia's easel covered over with a cloth. He wheeled over and peeked under the cloth then flipped it right off the painting.

"Holy smokes, Amelia! I didn't know you worked in oils." He gaped at the portrait of himself, his voice squeaking a bit as he added, "You even got some of my freckles in!"

Turning to Amelia, his face shining happily, he said, "WOW! It's great Amelia, I really like it."

Amelia's eyes started to fill up; she blushed, fumbling for her hanky.

Jean Paul raised her hand up in both of his as he leaned on his crutches.

"Madam, you are a very fine artist." He looked straight into her eyes and smiled.

Amelia seemed hypnotized, looking back into his grey-green eyes. She began to feel a bit strange.

"Amelia," Ben interrupted. "What do you think of the idea of drawing Jean Paul today? I already asked him and he's okay with it."

"Why, yes, yes, that's a good idea, Ben." She stammered a bit, then regained her composure and brought the cushioned chair beside her bed out for Jean Paul to sit on.

"I think if we sit him close to the window the light will be okay. Ben, what do you think?"

"Yeah, that's pretty good. Let's start out with charcoal until we get it right. Okay with you?"

"Fine." agreed Amelia.

Jean Paul sat down. Ben told him to turn his head a certain way, and to be quiet.

"We'll give you a break in 10 minutes, Jean Paul," Ben told him. The two artists then went to work sketching their new model.

He's got a good strong chin, Amelia thought as she looked at him. *His eyes are large and intelligent.*

Now how do I describe intelligence in a sketch? She wondered. *I'll 'organize my eyes' like Ben said, and maybe this will come out all right.*

After ten minutes, Jean Paul got up and stretched.

He asked Ben, "Is it all right if I see the sketches, Ben?"

Ben was still sketching but nodded his head, then said, "It's okay if you look at mine, but you'll have to ask Amelia."

Amelia gasped, still looking at her sketch. But Jean Paul was already heading towards her.

"Jean Paul, I'd rather you didn't see this right now. I'm a beginner at sketching and I'm not very pleased with this sketch. I'll let you see it when I'm happier with it."

Jean Paul laughed. "The sketch is probably just fine. It's the model who needs adjustment."

Amelia laughed softly. *Hmm, sense of humour,* she said to herself. She turned to Ben. "Let's have a cup of coffee or hot chocolate. What do you say, Ben?"

"Hot chocolate sounds great." Ben answered. "Do you have any more of those cookies you baked the other day?"

Ben wandered over to see Amelia's sketch, met Jean Paul's quizzical look and said, "It's okay if I look. I'm her sketch teacher. She's my painting teacher. We do a trade in art."

"Get over here and sit down at the table, Ben, and you, too, Jean Paul. I'm grateful for Ben who has been very patient with me. I love painting landscapes but never learned to sketch faces."

"Yah," added Ben. "And she never had any lessons either, like we get in school."

"How long have you been painting?" Jean Paul asked.

"Ever since I was a child. I love nature, all the seasons, all the different colours of the seasons."

"I have always wanted to sketch and paint. Would you two consider taking another student?"

Ben grinned. He turned to Amelia and said, "It's okay with me. What do you say, Amelia?"

CHAPTER 20

HILDA BURKHART AND THE "DROP IN A WHILE" TEA ROOM

OTTO BURKHART'S WIFE HILDA HAD REQUESTED A meeting with Betty and Dr. Allan Gregory, and the meeting was taking place at the Burkhart residence.

Hilda greeted them both warmly. "Both Otto and I were thrilled when we received your offers from the real estate company regarding the sale of Happy Days Retirement Home and Resident Care package." She explained as she took some papers out of her brief case.

"Let's sit down and talk about what has been going on in the home in the last year." Hilda indicated the couch for Betty and Allan and pulled out a padded chair for herself in front of them. She put her briefcase on the little side table beside the couch.

"We took the home off the market because we wanted to first have a meeting with you both to discuss the hopes we have for the retirement home and building."

Betty and Allan both looked at each other then back at Hilda who continued.

"First of all, we all have to understand many of the legalities only the lawyers can put down on paper, but what I want to know is, are you both still interested in the ownership of Happy Days Retirement Home?"

"Definitely I am, and even more so since Allan and I would be working in a partnership. We both have the same ideas regarding improvements in the home and care program." Betty answered immediately.

Allan smiled, his eyes twinkling. "It has been my greatest hope to be able to help the elderly, since I believe they deserve the best in their final years." Looking at Betty, he added, "I can't think of a finer partner than Betty here. She has some excellent ideas."

Opening her binder, Hilda took out and passed several papers to each of them, and kept the third copy for herself.

"Otto and I made a brief record of the ins and outs of what has been going on here in the residence for the last year. We want to go over this with both of you together."

Clearing her throat, she discussed the value of the residence structure, the improvements made, as well as the cost to update the apparent need areas. Then she went on to outline the cost of the 'care giving' aspect. Lastly she defined the amount of money coming in through client fees and donations.

Allan asked about the recent problem with Karl and how the money would be repaid.

"Karl has taken out a loan from the bank, and has repaid the amount he owed." She added, "Since this is a confidential meeting, I would like to add that Karl is receiving therapy for his addiction. He is not permitted to have any dealings with money in our establishment at any time."

Betty asked, "Have you had any thoughts regarding hiring a Recreation Therapist? I know this would assist the residents greatly in keeping their interests up and mixing socially both with each other as well as merging at times with the community."

"Yes, Betty. We have arranged to hire Lori, our nursing assistant, as soon as she graduates. She's taking Recreation Therapy in night school and will be excellent in the job. All the residents love her."

She smiled, thinking of Lori. "That means we will need to hire another nurse's assistant, and pay another salary for Lori. We have set aside an account for that. Lori graduates sometime in the next six months."

Indicating the papers, she said, "Everything is explained regarding the ins and outs of what has happened here in the last year."

Allan asked several more questions mostly about legislation in British Columbia as well as the Canadian Health Care system. Hilda answered what she could and mentioned that Betty, because she was more cognizant and current with recent legislation in the Health Care system, was a good resource for his questions.

Hilda rose. "I've got to run now. Otto wants me to get to the hospital and tell him all about our meeting. May I tell him you are both interested?"

"Yes." Betty and Allan answered together, then started to laugh at their verbal duet.

"Good," smiled Hilda. "Otto will be very pleased as I am already. Will you work with your lawyers, have them get in touch with our lawyer? We'll need your retainer cheques and after all the papers are signed, we can finalize everything. Then we can schedule the board meeting."

She stood up, and gathered her papers.

"Otto and I want to go on that cruise we booked a while ago. I want to make sure everything is down in black and white before we go."

Betty and Allan nodded their heads in agreement, looking happily astounded at what had transpired.

She smiled warmly, reached over and shook their hands, and then left the office, closing the door softly behind her.

Betty looked at Allan in amazement and said, "Am I dreaming or did you and I receive an offer to become the owners in partnership of the Happy Days Retirement Home?

"Blimey!" Allan stood up, grabbed Betty in dance position and waltzed her around the room.

"This is exactly what I was hoping for Betty! Let's get out of here and discuss this more without any interruptions. I know exactly where we can go, and they'll give us a good cup of tea, too."

They both excitedly left her office, Betty explaining to her secretary that they were taking off early for a short meeting and probably not be back that day. She left instructions to let the charge nurse know and to follow protocol if there was an emergency situation.

As they hurried down the corridor, walking close together, talking and laughing, the secretary watched them leave and smiled knowingly.

There's a little tea room off Goldstream Avenue called "*Drop In a While.*" and decorated like an English tea room. In the foyer you are warmly greeted by the hostess, and taken through a graceful, carved wooden arch into the beautifully English style tea room. On the right is the wood burning fireplace with two comfortable padded arm chairs placed in front it. Between the chairs is a round table with a white starched table cloth. Standing invitingly in its center is the typical silver three-tiered service, loaded with little dainty sandwiches, English scones, and on the top layer, bite sized cookies, butter tarts, and chocolates. There's usually a porcelain tea pot and a tea cup placed beside the tray. The table announces to all the tea room patrons its many culinary pleasures.

Scattered about the room are many round and oval tables with four chairs about them. Some are straight-backed wooden ones in antique designs and others are more padded chairs with padded arms. The lighting is subdued, and there is space between tables for the patrons to wander about and socialize.

When Betty and Allan entered the "Drop in a While," Betty was greeted and stopped briefly by one of her client's relatives. The cute blonde hostess spied Allan, and greeted him warmly with a big smile. She twinkled, "Welcome, Allan!" Then she added more softly and coquettishly, "Phone me, Allan," raising her eyebrows invitingly. Betty caught up to Allan at that moment. The hostess' face dropped as she realized that Allan had a lady friend with him. She blushed, then stage whispered, "Don't phone me, Allan," and turned to lead the couple into the tea room. She asked over her shoulder, "Your usual table, Allan?"

"No, we want the alcove in the corner. We need to talk." She ushered them both to a modest sized, comfortable looking niche with a round table and two padded chairs, a little secluded from the others.

The piano player was playing a choice of love songs that drifted softly around the room filling the atmosphere gently with warmth and congeniality.

When the waitress came, Betty ordered black coffee. The waitress brightened when Allan ordered a pot of tea, milk and sugar, and asked Betty if she was interested in cookies, scones or a sandwich. She shook her head, "Just coffee, Allan. Thanks."

"You do serve coffee here, don't you?" She asked the waitress who reassured her that they served very good coffee. When she left, the couple started discussing the weather and other mundane subjects as other patrons sauntered by, greeting Allan and looking at Betty quizzically. Some stopped to chat, forcing Allan to introduce Betty.

Their order arrived; they both found it difficult to get their thoughts together. Betty realized that their conversation held a lot of interest to the smiling people ambling by their table and suggested that they go to her office where there was complete privacy. Allan looked at his watch.

"It's almost time to go home, anyway, Betty."

"How about coming to my house for dinner?" Betty suggested.

"Great idea. I'll buy some wine on the way! White or red?"

They left together. Allan put his arm around Betty's shoulders as they went through the door, and the hostess sighed as she watched them go. The piano player cranked out a jazzy "Tea for Two" over a louder animated buzz of conversation.

CHAPTER 21

NEW CHOICES

AMELIA CALLED ME EARLY SATURDAY MORNING. "Margaret," she said firmly, "I'm getting restless to do something. I'd like to get a job, and after I do that I'll look for another apartment."

"Do you have any ideas as to where you want to work?" I asked.

"Vaguely," she replied.

"Maybe in a lawyer's office, doing what I did before, in Saskatchewan." She added, "It's been a long time since I worked, what with my Adam being sick for so long, and then my own illness."

I listened but gave no suggestions. This was her decision, unless she asked me.

"I was thinking of applying somewhere, working at a place that doesn't need much experience or training. When I get used to a working routine again, I'll look for something else. What do you think Margaret?"

Before I could answer, Amelia went on, "Maybe a fast food place as a cashier. I learned to handle an adding machine, and I know how to do books, and did a lot of that when I worked for the accountant."

"If you're serious about working, do you have a resume ready?" I asked.

"Sort of," she answered. I've written it out longhand and will ask Betty if I can use the secretary's typewriter after she's done for the day."

"Will you be happy as a cashier?" I asked.

"Oh, that's just to get me into a routine while I look for a real job. It'll help me put some money into my pocket, and give me an experience in talking to people in the community." She sighed and pressed on.

"It's till I find something in a place I know I would like. Today, I saw in the Goldstream Gazette an ad for a part-time secretary. I thought I'd take a taxi to that address and scout it out, before I answered the 'ad. I could then tell if I want to work there by sniffing-out the feeling in the office and talking to some employees, if possible."

Amelia amazed me with her planning abilities. Mind you, she always was a good planner, and efficient at whatever she chose to do.

"Have you discussed any of this with Betty?" I asked.

"Not yet. She's been busy having meetings with that new doctor, Allan Gregory."

"He told us all to call him 'Dr. Allan.' I guess he wants us to feel at ease with him. He's attended to us well, and the girls at my table adore him. He seems so happy these days; I'd swear he's in love."

I was about to ask her, "What are your ideas regarding getting prepared for interviews and all that, Amelia?"

She must have read my mind, because she went on, "I've been vising that Thrift store I told you about and gathered together some real nice working clothes. At the fast food or fast service businesses, I'd probably wear a uniform, but I'll need my new duds for the job I know how to do."

I smiled. Amelia sounded as if she was back to the real sharp Amelia of the old days.

"How's everything at the home?" I asked. "Are the art lessons going well with little Ben?"

"Oh my!" She paused.

I knew her well enough to think she was holding back something.

"Well, now I have two art students, little Ben is doing soooo well, and my new student, Jean Paul," she paused again. "He's that French Canadian fellow I mentioned a while ago."

"Why yes, Amelia, Betty told me all about him. He rooms next to you, doesn't he?" I asked innocently, probably with a twinkle in my eye.

"Well, he's simply marvelous at catching on. He will try anything and give it his best shot. He's better at water colours than at sketching, but sketching is a real art in itself."

"But what's he like, Amelia?".

"Now you stop it, Margaret, she said adamantly. "I know that teasing tone of voice of yours! Now I won't tell you anything more about Jean Paul." She paused.   We chatted a bit more about make-up and hair do's.

"Margaret, I have to go. Jean Paul said he'll be calling in about ten minutes. I want to be ready. Good talking to you. Come and see me soon, y'hear?

"Bye for now Margaret. Thanks for being there, for me," and she hung up.

CHAPTER 22

HANS BURKHART AND JEAN PAUL'S MOTORCYCLE

AFTER TALKING TO MARGARET, HER SISTER-IN-LAW, Amelia got dressed in the 'new to her' clothes, put on some make-up and brushed her hair again. She checked her image in the mirror, then sat and waited.

When Jean Paul knocked on Amelia's door, she leaped up to open it. He was simply beaming with excitement.

"Amelia, how pretty you look. Hans is downstairs waiting for us in his Dad's car. I am dying to see what he's done with my Harley. He's been working on it since the accident."

Amelia knew all about Hans and Craig. Jean Paul had taken them to meet Amelia after he arrived in the Happy Days home. She knew how they rescued Jean Paul last August.

Since Jean Paul and Amelia shared the same bathroom, he often left her notes inviting her out to see certain performances, or events. Their comings and goings together were observed with great interest by the older guests in the retirement home and they had been the subject of many lively dinner conversations.

"Jean Paul, this is exciting! To see your motorcycle again! I'm feeling your excitement, too. Let's take the elevator. Your leg isn't ready for stairs yet, is it?"

"No, I'd probably fall down. I want to get there so fast." Jean Paul took her arm and together they hurried, as fast as Jean Paul was able to hurry using his cane and hanging onto Amelia. Into the old, noisy elevator they went, and when Jean Paul leaned over to push the down button, his face touched Amelia's briefly. He noted that she did not turn her face away, and he smiled gently down to her, as the door closed. Then he took her face tenderly in one big hand and kissed her softly.

His face is radiant and his eyes are sparkling. Gosh he's so happy! He's so loveable and handsome.

Amelia felt her heart speeding up, and caught her breath. His body was warm against hers, and she felt herself responding to his closeness. That exquisitely warm delicious feeling began to rise up slowly and seductively inside her, radiating and pulsating from her very core.

My God! she thought, even my toes are curling!

Hans was at the curb holding the car door open for them. He, too, was grinning from ear to ear.

"Jean Paul, I can't wait till you see her! And I got a 95 percent mark on all the repairs that had to be done! My instructor is proud of me! Wow!"

Then turning to Amelia he asked, "Amelia, would you mind if I put you in the back seat, so I can explain to Jean Paul all about my repair job on the Harley?"

"No, not at all, Hans. It's an exciting day for both of you."

Amelia slid gracefully into the back seat, thinking to herself, *It'll give me a chance to cool down anyway.*

The trip took longer than expected because of early morning traffic, but Hans and Jean Paul were discussing the Harley in automotive language, which left Amelia free to relish and day-dream about her quest for a job but mostly to imagine what could have been, in the elevator ride with Jean Paul.

He turned often to look at her, and to smile softly.

At the technical school, Hans took charge, leading them proudly through the school to the mechanics lab. There he introduced them to his instructor.

The sleek, black, highly polished Harley motorcycle had been proudly placed on a pedestal beside the instructor's desk, for all the mechanics students to see. There was a sign leaning beside the front tire that read, Admire but don't touch.

A very large "before" photo leaned forlornly on the floor beside the pedestal's support.

"I wanted all my students to see what could be done if a student put his mind to it," explained the instructor.

"Hans told me all about your accident, Jean Paul" he said, adding, "Your lucky stars must have been looking out for you that day. Otherwise you might have died in that ravine!"

"Yes." Jean Paul smiled quietly looking at Hans. His eyes and voice were full of emotion. "God sent me two angels in disguise, riding on a motorcycle."

CHAPTER 23

AMELIA TRIES HER WINGS

UP IN NANAIMO, I WAS HAVING A CUP OF COFFEE WHILE reading the newspaper. It was early Saturday morning, when the phone jangled on the coffee table. I probably smiled, because I knew it was Amelia calling with her latest news from Victoria. It was.

"Margaret! So much has happened since we last spoke! Do you have time for me right now?"

I reassured her that I had time and asked, "Yes Amelia, but these calls are costing you a lot in long distance rates, aren't they?"

"Never mind that, Margaret! It's less expensive than travelling up to Nanaimo, every time I have some news. I have so much to tell you."

She was bubbling with excitement.

"First of all, I was hired by that lawyer, Bob Stevenson who I went to see about the job offered in the newspaper. Margaret! He hired me! I got that job! I'll be his secretary. Then I looked for an apartment near the job. And..." Her excitement spilled over.

"Guess what? Your friend Betty knows the son of a client who died here recently and he is renting his dad's house out. I went to look at it. It's perfect for me if I get someone to come in with me and pay half the rent."

"Have you put an ad in the Victoria gazette?"

"Not yet. When I mentioned it to Jean Paul, he insisted on looking at the house and wants to come in with me to share it. He's sick of living in Happy Days like I am."

"Amelia, how's that going to look to everyone, you living with a man you aren't married to? People will say you are.... living in sin...so to speak."

"Let them talk, Margaret. My new boss says he's taking time off in Africa next month, and hopes to close up the office when he's gone. The only person to stay there will be the receptionist. He's paid me already. I thought I'd do some travelling too, maybe take a tour to Norway, to connect with my mother's relatives there. Another thought I had while browsing through the travel magazine Bob gave me was to travel to South America, with a tour and climb part of Machu Picchu, that famous mountain in Peru."

"My goodness, Amelia, where are you getting all this money?"

"I know. It's expensive, but Adam's life insurance was more than I expected. And my mother left me a sizeable amount that Dad had invested years ago, which grew all the while she lived with us. It was another big surprise when I talked to my investment counsellor."

"What about the house you are renting?"

"Maybe Jean Paul will take care of the house while I'm gone. Whatever happens after that between us, I cannot predict right now."

I heard her clear her throat before she went on.

"Margaret, it's not like Jean Paul and I are two kids you know. Now I think when I return he will probably be well enough, and strong enough to ride his motorcycle back to Quebec."

"Well, Amelia, you sure sound like you are getting all your marbles together again. If you find another love interest as you go along, you are certainly due a happier life now that you're well. What do your kids say about all this?"

"Now, I haven't said anything to the children about him. I did say I was looking for a house. They all told me to get a house with room for them when they come to visit."

"Well, Amelia, now that you're almost out of the Happy Days, how about taking the bus up here to Nanaimo, and spending the week with me? I'm off work all next week and would love to see you again. We could take in some of the sights. The weather is good right now, and I'd like to see you again. We can talk a lot more about things without you getting more long distance charges on your phone."

"Yes, we could do that, I'm sure." Amelia sounded very thoughtful. "But remember, Margaret, I'm not the dumb dodo I was when I was sick."

She giggled a little. "I won't be letting you try and talk me out of anything like you used to when we were kids, remember?"

This time, I'm going to take care of me, and do all the things I used to dream about doing.

CHAPTER 24

AN IMPORTANT MEETING

DR. OTTO BURKHART AND HIS WIFE HILDA CALLED A meeting of Happy Days board, and included Betty Armstrong and Dr. Allan Gregory. This meeting took place in the Burkhart's home. As the people arrived, they were very graciously welcomed by both Otto and Hilda Burkhart, then ushered into the large living room.

Fire was crackling warmly in the fireplace, and Hilda had coffee, tea, and cookies prepared and waiting on her tea wagon.

"Come on, everyone! Have a cup of coffee. She gestured at the teapot, then pointed to Allan with a fond smile, "Allan, there's tea for you and anyone else who wants it."

"Karlie, darling, come pass around the cookies! They're your favourite."

Karlie was her name for Karl Jr. her oldest grandson. Hilda and Otto had called the meeting to explain to the board about the new changes in ownership of Happy Days Retirement Home. They wanted to explain the reason for their resignation as owners. They also wanted to introduce Betty and Allan, the new investors, and to explain to the board about the new arrangements for the running and dispersal of ownership shares that had been implemented.

The group had a little social time, then Otto called the meeting to order.

"As you know, Hilda and I plan to do some extensive travelling. We, therefore, drew up with our lawyer a change in the ownership. Allan and Betty have invested a considerable sum, and hold the majority of shares at the moment. The rest of the shares are owned by us, as well as you Karl, Adolph, and Karl Jr. as part of your inheritance. Now, it may not be to your immediate liking, but we feel that in the best interest in the home, this dispersal of shares will mean the home will be run more efficiently and the residents will benefit in the long run."

He spoke of how the shares would be dispersed. "Hilda and I will hold between us 25%. Next, Betty Armstrong and Allan Gregory will hold 25% as they have invested a very large amount in the home. They agreed to buy out Otto and Hilda's shares in the next two years.

The investments for Karl and Adolph, 10% each, while grandson Karl Jr. will have 5%."

He held up his hand to quieten his two sons. "Let us continue. The Residents will certainly benefit from the medical expertise of both Betty and Allan, besides bringing their knowledge and honesty to oversee that everything will be done legally. We, Hilda and I, will be assured that Happy Days will live on after we die."

"All board members will continue to be paid and Betty Armstrong and Allan Gregory will be required to sit with the board and have full voting rights. Otto rose, put his hand on Hilda's shoulder, a silent hint for her to sit down.

He then continued, "For your further information, the financial theft by Karl of thousands of dollars is being attended to by Karl under the supervision of our legal treasurer, and one of the terms of repayment is that Karl receive counselling. Karl has made arrangements for this to our satisfaction and will be monitored by Dr. Gregory."

He gave each person a copy of the new ownership agreements. He asked them all to read the papers before he added, "Again, I stress that should anyone wish to bring this matter to the courts, then both Karls will be charged. For your own safety, I hope you will accept our terms and keep the peace." He took time to regard each of his family before speaking further.

"I have invited our lawyer, legal treasurer, and two members of the staff of Happy Days Retirement Home to be witnesses to your signatures. They are waiting in the other room." Are there any questions?"

"Yes Otto, I have one." Allan Gregory stood up and asked, "How are you and Hilda going to be part of our meetings if you are in Peru, South America, or some other mysterious continent?"

The Burkharts smiled, then Hilda answered.

"Both of us will be checking up on how things are going.

"Dad, I could take your spot while you are gone," said Karl. "I know I made a horrible mistake in the past, but I know I would be fair to everyone."

"Thanks, Karl," said Otto, "But I've left that decision to Allan and Betty, right now. They are the major investors. However, Hilda and I won't be going for long periods. I'm sure whatever decision has to be made if there is a tie, the situation will wait until our return."

Hilda interjected.

"The time is running out and our visitors are waiting. Shall I invite them in to witness all our signatures?"

Karl rose and said, "Definitely, Mom and Dad, for me it is a new page that I've turned."

The rest of the members nodded their heads.

Otto went to get the witnesses. Their lawyer took over the instructions as to where each witness should sign, and the documents were signed.

Karl shook hands with Allan cordially.

With Betty, he shook hands, and muttered in her ear quietly, "Betty, please forgive me for being such a lout."

Betty grinned, stood on her toes and said in Karl's ear, "You are forgiven, Karl. If it ever happens again, I just may sock you right in the schnoz!"

They both laughed and he said, "I'll sure be careful then, Betty. They say my nose is my best feature."

CHAPTER 25

NEW ARRANGEMENTS

"MARGARET, I'M MOVING TOMORROW, SO I'LL BE BUSY for a-while getting things I need for the house." Amelia was talking to Margaret on the phone. She had signed a lease on the house she rented with Jean Paul.

The couple was moving out of Happy Days Retirement Home. Amelia was now working for a lawyer, and Jean Paul was accepted to teach at the University of Victoria.

"I know, maybe I'm rushing this romance, but heavens, Margaret, neither of us are kids anymore; we do know what we're doing and have been around the block more than a few times." She frowned, hearing admonitions to wait from Margaret.

"No, Margaret, our minds are made up. In fact, I know I love him. However, I also want to do a few things for myself. Like go to Peru! I'll be gone about ten days."

She took a deep breath. "You know, Margaret, I'm done with grieving. This is my life, and I'm not going to sit around forever feeling sorry for my losses. I've been given a new birth, and I'm taking my second breath at life!"

She laughed when Margaret said, "I've said all I'm supposed to say if I was your mother. As your friend, let me paraphrase, have a wonderful time."

CHAPTER 26

BELIEVE! NEVER, NEVER GIVE UP! 1961

LITTLE BEN HAD BEEN TAKING AND ALSO GIVING ART lessons with Amelia for quite some time now. They had formed a powerful bond. As fellow artists, Ben had formed a real strong relationship with Jean Paul too. When he came to the house the couple had rented, he was full of excitement.

"Hey, Jean Paul, thanks for all the martial arts lessons you've given me. You know that kid in my class? Well, that kid has finally stopped bothering me. The last time he came up and tried to tip me over, I did what you said, and grabbed him like this!" Ben demonstrated the move he had learned from Jean Paul.

"But you know what happened? First of all, I got him down but me and my wheel chair, I call him "Steve", fell right on top of him! He could not move. I had him pinned right down to the ground!" Ben demonstrated again.

"I said to him, 'How do you like that?' And you know what? He started to cry. Then the principal got me off'n him and we both had to stay after school for fightin' in the school yard."

Jean Paul laughed but became very thoughtful as he replied, "Well, you did the right thing. But remember you only use martial arts when you are attacked, and need to protect yourself. You never attack anyone using anything I've taught you."

"Okay, Jean, my friend and buddy. But I wanted to ask you something. When we both went over, me on top of him, that was okay, wasn't it?

"Yes, it's part of using your energy force, and gravity to protect yourself."

"Well, a funny thing happened to me then. I got a cramp in my left leg. Honest! I really felt it cramp! I know, the doctor said I would never feel anything again. But I felt that cramp!" His face screwed up with the memory.

"Hmm, I wonder?" mused Jean Paul. "Maybe we should talk to our friend Dr. Gregory. I'll find out when he could see you and we'll tell your dad and mom about it right away."

"Oh, they know about it. When I told them what I felt, they seemed excited for some reason and called Dr. Gregory right away. We'll see him this afternoon." Ben said in a matter of fact voice.

"Do you think there's a chance it's good news?"

Jean Paul listened intently before replying. "Where there's feeling, even if it's a cramp, there's always hope, mon amie. Keep up your hopes. You know, they told me I would not use this leg again, at the knee, and were ready to amputate. I said, 'No! Wait', give me a chance to work with it,' and sure enough, now I am walking on both legs."

"I only limp when I'm tired, and am working every day to correct that. Bien sûr! It takes time and practice, but with God on your side, everything is possible."

Jean Paul put his hand on Ben's shoulder, smiling a bit and said, "I am proud of you for taking care of yourself with that bully."

Ben smiled, pulling a piece of paper from his pocket. "This is just a cartoon, but I thought you would like it."

The sketch was of Ben and Steve the wheelchair, on the ground on top of an obese fellow. Ben had written on the bottom of the cartoon, 'A comfortable pillow.'

Adam and Karla, Ben's parents, had already taken Ben to a specialist who was very dubious about the cramp Ben had felt. Karla was a kinesiologist and had been exercising Ben's legs ever since the accident.

When Dr. Allan Gregory examined Ben, he was very thoughtful.

"Ben," he said after he had seen Ben the second time, "Do you think you have a chance to walk again?"

Ben raised his shoulders, put his hands up, and said, "The other doctor said no. I don't know what to think. I never thought much about it."

"Do you want to walk again?" Allan asked.

"Yes. I do. But I thought I didn't ever have a chance."

"Your mom has been working every day on those legs of yours. They are in good shape because of her, not withered at all. They have even grown with you."

"Okay, then, I'm going to walk again" said Ben flatly. "If I could beat the bully, I can do this, too. But I'll miss old Steve, my trusty wheelchair. He's always been my good buddy." He patted the arms of his wheelchair.

Later, there were quite a few people concerned with Ben in Dr. Gregory's office. Dr. Gregory was thoughtful again before he said, "Ben, I've worked with many injured men during the war. Some had damaged legs and they never walked again. But some of them had similar injuries. Those men scoffed at the possibility of being wheelchair bound. They worked and worked and worked, exercising and getting strength back. Eventually, they walked again. I often wonder if healing starts by first saying I will heal. Then working, exercising and believing."

He seemed to be lost in memories before he straightened and added, "You know, if you think you can, then you will. But if you think you can't, then you won't."

Ben scratched his head "That sounds about right. I'm gonna walk. Yes, I'm gonna walk, even if it kills me!' and added, but it won't kill me. Hey! I may even fly, like my Dad."

Karla smiled, and ruffled Ben's hair. "We certainly have been working towards that end, Ben. And it won't kill you. When we do all your morning exercises, I've noticed your legs are getting more flexible and the muscles are getting bigger. I, too, have seen people get better when all the odds were against them. Yes, I believe it's all about never giving up hope."

Dr. Allan Gregory smiled at them all. "Guess if we all believe he will walk, that life energy of all of us will count for something too. Remember Ben, we all have faith in what you're going to do to succeed."

He got up, filled several paper cups with water, and passed them out to each one. Let's have a toast to Ben walking again!"

They all toasted. "To Ben's success in learning to walk again!"

CHAPTER 27

ANOTHER NEW BEGINNING, 1962

BEN ASKED HIS FRIEND JEAN PAUL TO COME TO SCHOOL
with him. His teacher had been very interested in Ben's report of
the bullying, and asked if Ben had received any lessons in martial
arts. That's when Ben told him all about Jean Paul, and agreed to
bring him to meet the teacher.

"Jean Paul, I want you to meet some of my friends at school.
And the teacher wants to talk to you, too. Everyone wants to meet
you after I threw the bully down. Will you come tomorrow with
me? And ya' know what? They think I'm a hero! Can you imagine
that? I'm a real hero!" Ben thumped his chest like Tarzan and bel-
lowed a war cry.

Jean Paul grinned. "Sure, mon amie, I'll come. You want me to
drive you instead of taking the bus?"

"Okay, but I'll have to let the driver know or he'll worry."

"What time?

"About 8:15. That'll give me a chance to show you around."

When they arrived at school, there was a large cluster of Ben-sized boys waiting for them. They surrounded the car, peering in on tip toe at Jean Paul. Ben rolled down the window and proudly commanded the little mob, "Get back fellows, let my guy breathe. Hey! We want to get out." The boys fell back a few paces to let Jean Paul open the doors without hurting them.

Jean Paul received a barrage of questions as he unpacked Ben's wheelchair, and placed it beside the car. Reaching in to carry his young friend, Ben whispered in his ear, "I want to show you something, Jean buddy. Watch my left leg."

Still in Jean Paul's arms and his arms around Jean's neck, Ben concentrated mightily, and the left leg straightened slightly, enough for Jean Paul to howl in glee, "Buddy! Ben, buddy, you did it! You did it! All by yourself, you did it!"

"I know I did it. That weren't no old twitch, it was me who made it move!"

The group of boys fell quiet, then shouted "Do that again, Ben!"

Jean Paul waded through the crowd of young folks and carried Ben to his chair, but instead of strapping the belt around his legs, so they wouldn't twitch, he simply put his big hands on Ben's thighs and asked Ben, "Can you do that sitting down, Ben?"

Ben concentrated; his little face screwed up with effort, and the foot began to rise about three inches, then fell back down. "When Mom sees that, I betcha she'll have me in the gym all day!"

Jean Paul smiled and put the strap around his legs, in case there was any more uncontrolled twitching. Then he turned his attention to all the questions being thrown at him about martial arts training.

Ben's teacher had been watching with great interest from the classroom window. He smiled as he went out to meet what he hoped would be the new martial arts teacher.

When Jean Paul picked Ben up from school, Karla was already there and she was beaming, and could hardly contain herself.

"Jean Paul, I think we have a miracle boy on our hands now. I heard all about what happened this morning. Praise God, I think our boy is going to walk! He is determined! Oh my goodness, I think he's going to walk. Thank God!

In the following weeks Karla worked even harder to keep Ben's legs moving. Jean Paul had told Dr. Gregory about Ben's progress, and they had arranged for a trainer in rehabilitation to help.

About three weeks later, Ben and Dr. Allan were talking about the trainer's exercises, Jean Paul asked Ben, "Would it be okay with you if we asked you to stand up, Ben? We'll help you get up if you like. We want to see how much your mom has helped to maintain your muscles."

"Sure, Jean Paul, I'd like to know, too." replied Ben.

Dr. Allan asked, "Ben, do your legs twitch as much as they used to after the accident? Have you noticed any difference?"

"Yes, I have doctor. It's been getting less. You see, Mom works with my legs every morning. I never thought about it much, but now that you ask me, it doesn't twitch as much," Ben replied.

They were in Dr. Allan Gregory's office. He cleared away the chairs, making a wide arc around them. Jean Paul released the belt around Ben's thighs.

"Does he need this anymore, Allan?"

Ben was quiet before asking, "Hey, doctor Allan, I always wondered why they twitched. You got an answer?"

Dr. Allan smiled at him. "Ben, you always amaze me." He pulled one of the chairs back and sat down beside him.

"Here goes, Ben. It's a long explanation and I want you to ask questions if you don't understand." He put an arm around him.

"After you were hit by that drunk driver, the blow injured your spine. The nerve cells below where you were hit became disconnected from your brain at the level of your injury. Then scar tissue formed, blocking messages from below the injury spot from getting to the brain. Your body went into spinal shock that could last from several weeks to a much longer time. The fact that your mom kept up exercises, means that the scar tissue gradually became less and less. I believe a doctor prescribed some pills to help reduce the spasticity of your legs, didn't he?

"I have to take two pills, but they were cut down to one lately."

"Well. Your own efforts to re-establish a connection, your youth, plus the efforts of your mom to keep up range of motion exercises have helped you to regenerate real muscle tone in your legs. It has also begun to establish a real connection to your brain through the spine."

"Holy smokes, doctor Allan, that's a lot for me to think about." He cleared his throat, his facial expression becoming intense with tears. "I sure hope I can walk again. Yeah, I sure hope I can walk again. Jean Paul says miracles happen with a lot of hope, prayer, and energy, sometimes the energy of many." He wiped his eyes roughly with his arm. Then he said, "Let's begin, okay?"

Just then, Amelia stuck her head into the office. "May I come in? I want to see my Ben do his thing."

The day was Saturday, Amelia had the time off. Ben replied, "Come on in Amelia! Let's all work on me at once. All our energy together will make everything work! I read that in the book I got from the library."

Ben's facial expressions showed he was concentrating hard. He said, "Don't do anything until I tell you, okay?"

Amelia placed one hand in little Ben's. "You can do this, Ben."

Ben ordered the group, "You get me up when I tell you and don't let go of me until I tell you. I'll count to three, at three, get me up and I'll count again. You stop holding me after another count of three."

Dr. Allan gently took one arm while Jean Paul grabbed the other. Ben commanded firmly, "One, two, three, NOW!"

They pulled little Ben into a standing position.

"We've got you steady, Ben. Now, count again."

"One, two, three!"

Ben stood by himself, weaving some, for almost 30 seconds before he started to wobble. The men caught him as he started to crumble.

Dr. Allan's voice wavered with emotion. "Ben, you are getting stronger every day. Keep working with the therapist and Karla. Never, never, never give up! You are going to walk again. It will take time, as much as you need. Keep up the good work. You are a real miracle!"

Ben leaned back into his wheelchair and a sob escaped from his usually tougher expression. After a minute, he said with a slight impish glint in his eyes, "Hey, everyone, first I'm a hero and now I'm a miracle. Be careful or I'll get a swelled head!" They all laughed and Amelia hugged Jean Paul, who then leaned down and put his big hands on Ben's head. "Ben, you will someday wear a black belt. But today you earned six of them."

CHAPTER 29

A TOUR TO SOUTH AMERICA, 1964

"I'M GOING TO SIGN UP FOR THAT TOUR TO PERU," AMELIA said over the newspaper to Jean Paul. They had finished dinner; it was Friday evening and they had decided to stay home, instead of going to their favourite movie house.

"You mean the one in yesterday's paper? That's the one I want to take. I was going to invite you to think of coming along."

They looked at each other and started to laugh.

"Are we already reading each other's thoughts?" Amelia asked. "I thought that happened only to old married couples."

The tour was scheduled to take place in three weeks. When Jean Paul phoned to make arrangements, he was given all the information and told to get his application in as soon as possible.

The couple scrambled to fill out forms, check their immunization status, get vaccinated, and pack their bags. Fortunately, they both had passports, and in record time they were ready to take their tour of Peru, Ecuador, and Columbia.

They arranged with the Wheeler family to watch their house, take in the mail and gave them Margaret's telephone number, to contact if there was any problem. However, Margaret insisted in coming down to see them off. She stayed with the Wheelers overnight, and they all went to the bus station to see the couple off with good wishes.

"Remember, don't eat the fresh fruit unless they're bananas or oranges, or a fruit you have to peel." Margaret cautioned. "When I was there, I spent most of my time in bed with Montezuma's revenge from eating whatever I wanted."

"I can only wish you good health and plenty of it," she added, hugging them both.

From the Wheelers, they received big, medium-sized and smaller hugs from each member, and then were off on the first leg of their trip.

That bus took them to the ferry that would cross to Tsawwassen on the BC mainland, and then take them over to meet the tour at Vancouver's airport.

It was about a month after they had left that Margaret received this letter.

Tuesday, May 28th, 1964

Dear Margaret

We have already visited Ecuador and Columbia and are winding up our tour in Peru. We like Peru the best. In Lima, the capital, we visited a small distill-ery to see how the country's drink called Pisco is made. The government strictly regulates making that drink, demanding that Pisco be made by only developing the pure expression of the grapes and only in small batches. They don't add water or sugar or any addi-tives whatsoever. It is aged only in glass or stainless steel, but is never aged in wood which would alter its flavour. I found it a pleasant enough drink, and it sure was strong in it's effect on my head! We're bringing you a bottle of Pisco Pur. But I warn you, sip a little at a time or it may knock you off your feet!

May 29, 1964

Dear Margaret,

Today is Wednesday. We are taking a plane early this morning to Cusco, in the mountains. When we got to the airport, we saw the small plane that was to take us there. The pilot was standing by his plane welcoming us, and guess what! He had an orange tabby cat under his arm. He said the cat was for Buenas Suerte, "Good Luck", and we flew over some pretty high mountains before we arrived in Cusco. There we were to stay overnight and acclimatize to the thinner air and height of the mountain. They served us Mate tea as soon as we got to the hotel which is supposed to help with altitude sickness. We saw something amazing on the street there. A native man was carrying a piano on his back, moving it from one house to another further down the same street. Our guide said he drankMate Tea, which gave him great strength. He also said that the native mountain people who lived there all the time had great chest expansion, from breathing the thinner air, and that gave them the low, reverberating singing voice, which is typical of their region.

May 30th, 1964. Thursday night

Dear Margaret,

I'm excited, Margaret I can hardly get the facts straight on this wonderful day I'll start at the beginning, but I'm almost jumping out of my skin!

This morning we took the train to Agua Calientes. There was such a crowd of tourists around waiting, I thought we would never get on that train. Some of the people decided to take a hotel and come the next morning. But there were still too many people. But our reservations from the tour granted us special acceptance. The train winds its way around the mountain sometimes very close to the RIO Urubamba. Within a few hours we were at the station in Agua Caliente. Many of the tourists went to stay overnight in a hotel there, but we wanted to take the bus. We were lucky to get on the bus, again thanks to the tour captain.

Machu Picchu is magnificent in all its structural development. It has fresh running water through long stone canals to a reservoir. The simple buildings are all made of stone. They even have a huge flat stone called the Altar of the Condor, where sacrifices were done as well as where they laid out their dead to dehydrate in the sun. There were places where they grew gardens, and even a small building for a jail. Our guide spoke good English. He said there was more than one belief as to how Machu Picchu was built. One popular idea is that Machu Picchu was built by aliens. I can certainly relate to that one because the fresh running water travels right through the middle of those stone block canals in a straight line to the reservoir. This notion of aliens is rejected by the present Peruvians. Maybe they want to claim the settlement idea for themselves.

After the tour, we were allowed to wander around a bit. I wanted to see how steep the drop-off was coming up to the settlement. And here's where my life changed! I stood at the edge of that mountain settlement and looked around and then way down. If anyone had pushed me I would be gone. What an odd feeling as I looked below. The terrain on that steep descent was rocky with small trees growing out from the sides of that mountain. They sprouted very sharply, their trunks bent out then up like a perpendicular arm bent up towards the sun. Jean Paul put a hand on my arm and pulled me away from the edge into the clearing again. He said, "Don't take chances up here; I don't want to lose you!" Then he leaned over and kissed me, pulled out a ring from his pocket, got on his knee and asked me to marry him. WOW! Margaret, I still feel breathless as I remember that moment!

"Yes" I said, and hugged and kissed him back. My heart was hammering as if I'd run the marathon, or climbed straight up that Machu Picchu mountain. I know we both love each other very much. It feels good to be loved like Jean Paul loves me. French men are more demonstrative, and it feels sooooo good to be loved by him. Ummmmm Hummm Will write more tomorrow.

CHAPTER 30

FRIDAY, MAY 31, 1964

Dear Margaret,

Jean Paul has the ability to keep everything in order, and tell me what he thinks without giving me a hard time. He's funny too, and makes me laugh a lot.

I can say I love him, without loving Adam any less. I think with love there's always room for more loving, and I know Adam would approve. He doesn't come to see me anymore, but I can sense his approval.

The funny thing was that after I said I'd marry Jean Paul, I was sure I saw Adam in the little crowd wandering about on Machu Picchu. He was smiling. I saw him for a second and then he was gone.

But Listen! About the same time I saw Adam, Jean Paul said he thought he that felt his first wife Angela touch him on the shoulder. When he turned to face her, he said that she smiled at him, and disappeared.

Do you think they both came to give us their blessings? That's what I think and so does Jean Paul. What a revelation for us! We both think that life never ends; it becomes a different dimension.

Yesterday, our guide asked if anyone in the tour had seen anything strange. Hans, a nice fellow on the tour, said he thought he'd seen a ghost of the past.

The tour guide smiled and told us. "It is said that people from history are seen lingering here. I know one lady said she'd seen the emperor Pachacuti. She described him and it sounded very accurate."

Jean Paul and I looked at each other and I couldn't help crying. I saw him wipe his cheek, too; I guess we were both very moved that our late spouses had come way up there to give us their blessings.

Margaret, I have never been so happy. Jean Paul and I are looking forward to returning to Victoria to begin our new lives together. I am taking another breath at life, almost like being born again and starting to breathe without pain or grief, just a "love of living again".

On our way back we saw the moonlight on the Rio Urubamba. It flowed and fell in waterfalls of pure molten silver – beautiful beyond words. What a gorgeous memorable, heavenly day.

See you soon, much love to you.

CHAPTER 30

THE WEDDING AND HONEYMOON

WHEN THE HAPPY COUPLE RETURNED FROM SOUTH America to Victoria, they visited Margaret and told her all about their tour. Then Amelia said casually, "Oh, by the way Margaret, we want you to be the maid of honour at our wedding.

Jean Paul is going to ask Hans and Craig to be his best men.

Jean Paul asked Hans and later Craig to come to his home. When he asked them to be his best men, they almost cried, they were both honoured.

"What about you, Amelia?" Margaret asked. " Who will be your second attendant, since Jean Paul has two?"

Amelia replied, "Let me think about it, Margaret, and I'll let you know. I would have asked my daughter, Sarah, but she's due for another baby any time now and her doctor has advised her to stay where she is, and not travel. Apparently, she has experienced some problems with this pregnancy and he is worried about her."

Then I asked Betty Armstrong, but she was booked for a vacation and wouldn't even be here. She did suggest we book the reception in Happy Day's recreation room and that Lori would take care of all the arrangements."

The following Saturday Amelia mentioned to Margaret casually in their weekly phone conversation. "I've decided on my second attendant, Margaret."

"Well?" Margaret said, and waited for Amelia, who had paused.

"Why, I've asked "Not so Little Ben", she replied, and added, "Do you know what he said when I asked him?"

"No, but I can probably guess." Margaret answered with a wry tone

"He said, "Sure, Amelia, but do I have to wear a dress?""

The wedding of Amelia Archer and Jean Paul Laval took place on March 26th, 1964 at 10.00 am in the side room to the chapel of Centennial United Church. This room was used for smaller more intimate weddings. In attendance were the couple's dear friends and associates. The ladies group of the church had decorated the room beautifully.

In the simple, quiet ceremony, the couple spoke their own beautifully written pledges. When Jean Paul looked at Amelia, he thought, *She isbeautiful! Her face shines in happiness like the warmth in my heart. I am a lucky man.*

The Happy Days Retirement Home staff provided delicious food and beverages during the reception. They even had a small band that provided dance music. All the resident clients and the wedding guests had a wonderful time.

Although it was an unusual time to fly to Alaska, Jean Paul's father had asked them to go, since he lived there and wanted to meet Amelia and give them both his blessings. They were to leave the next day, March 27 on the 7:30 pm flight. Jean Paul taught his last class of that semester in the morning.

At 4:30 March 27 they were all packed and ready when Adam, Karla, and Ben picked them up in their station wagon. Regulations demand meant they were to be at the airport 2 hours before their flight because it was an international flight.

"I'm excited!" Amelia said. "I've always wanted to see Alaska and they say it's a wonderful place. What's your father like? Are you excited to see him again?"

"Yes, but I'm wondering if we're going too early." answered Jean Paul. "Their winters are tough ones and spring doesn't come early like in Victoria. It's strange, but I have this foreboding feeling in my gut."

They were off with much hugging and best wishes from Adam, Karla and Ben. Being early, but before they had even gone to check in, they heard a loud voice blasting over the public address system, "For all those going to Alaska, flight 203 has been cancelled!"

The couple looked at each other in amazement.

"Mon Dieu!" Jean Paul exclaimed.

"What's going on?" Amelia.

"We're not sure," said a uniformed attendant who was standing by the ticket agent's counter. He explained, "They may be having a storm or something around Alaska." He added, "There's been warnings of something happening from people monitoring the weather up there."

Amelia and Adam sat down and waited for another announcement, hoping for more information.

After discussing the flights, they decided to approach the ticket counter. The agent there told them what she knew about the cancellation.

"Can we change our ticket for someplace else?" Jean Paul held up their reservations. Then he added, "We are going on our honeymoon!"

She looked through her papers, made a phone call, brightened up and said, "There's a flight that leaves for the Bahamas in about 40 minutes. It was full, but at noon there were two last minute cancellations. One of the couples got ill and can't come. The two seats are for First Class, and include a two week stay in a resort in the Caribbean. Those seats are still open and the agent said to give you a 65% discount since its last minute. There's a refueling stop over in Toronto, and you stay overnight there, but the next morning you are off again! Are you interested? I've been there. It's fabulous for a honeymoon!" She winked at Paul and added, "Seeing the ocean, and sunshine! And go fishing!"

The couple looked at each other. He raised his eyebrows in a question, and Amelia nodded in a big enthusiastic yes back to him.

They transferred their tickets, were directed to another gate, and they and their luggage were on their way shortly after the change in plans.

"Maybe we can shop in Toronto for more appropriate clothes for this journey." Amelia breathed into Jean's ear.

"Oh boy, here we go!" Jean Paul answered.

Amelia and Jean Paul later learned that a huge 9.2 earthquake hit Alaska. Less than 4 hours after they left for the Bahamas, the first waves of a tsunami reached the outer coast of Vancouver Island. The Pacific Ocean rose to such high abnormal levels, that Port Alberni was ravaged by the flooding waters, causing horrible damage to ships and property alike.

However, the couple was oblivious to the happenings in Alaska, and knew nothing about what might have happened to Jean Paul's father.

Their airline tickets included a package deal for a resort. What they had bought through the ticket attendant was an all-inclusive transaction in Nassau, in the Caribbean at a resort hotel on Paradise Island. The Royal Bahamian Hotel is famous for its grandeur.

The second lap of the journey saw them up at 4:30 in the morning with added luggage and a quick breakfast at the Toronto airport. When they arrived in Nassau, the many travelers in the new tour group they had joined were taken straight to their destination.

Amelia and Jean Paul were both dumbfounded by the luxury and elegance of their surroundings outside the hotel. The lush gardens with beautiful flowers of all sizes shapes and colours were enclosed by trees alive with chirping, twittering birds. They were as amazing in their different hues and shades as the gorgeous ground covers beneath them.

"Wow," said Amelia. "Are we in heaven?" Jean Paul simply smiled, put his arm around her again and said, "No, we are in a beautiful oceanic country! Oh, ma belle amour! We are going to have such a wonderful time here."

Their hotel room looked out over a blue-green ocean. The manager who greeted them explained, "We gave you the ocean view room that was reserved. How fortunate for you! The clients who had reserved this room cancelled this morning. Then a few hours later we were alerted that you both were coming. Lucky break, for you!"

When he heard that Jean Paul and Amelia were honeymooning he shook their hands vigorously in congratulation. "I have just the gift for you both. Stay here a moment and I'll be right back!"

When he returned, he clutched in his hand a bunch of tickets some for fishing excursions, two for snorkeling, and two more for massage and spas. "This," he said, handing Jean Paul the tickets, "will get you both started on the 'time of your lives' here in the Caribbean!"

Their room had every luxury the couple could imagine.

"Come on, Jean Paul, let's go swimming!" Amelia had unpacked their things and put everything away in drawers and the closet. She held up their new bathing suits.

"Let's go swimming!" she caroled again. Away they went in brand new swim suits, down to the white sands to enjoy the sunshine and turquoise waters.

It was very late that night when they were ready for bed. They were both exhausted, having met many in the tour, spent a long time on the beach, gotten their first sunburns, eaten delicious dinners, and danced to the rousing rhythms of the Caribbean dance band. When they reached their room, Jean Paul opened the window. They leaned on the window still mesmerized by the quiet magic of the waves caressing the shore. The ocean reflected the full moon and stars on the now black waters.

"Tell me, Jean Paul, darling, do you still have that nasty feeling in the pit of your stomach?"

Jean Paul laughed as he swung her into his arms and buried his face in her breasts, "No, belle fille, but now I have other very strong feelings. Let's go to bed, eh?"

After snuggling, then more passionate love making, they nodded off into a sleep that enclosed them both in a glow of loving all-embracing happiness and bliss.

CHAPTER 31

MARGARET'S MOVE TO CHEMAINUS, 1968

MARGARET PHONED AMELIA AND JEAN PAUL AT 8:30 Saturday morning on April 15,1968. Her voice sounded full of stress which concerned Amelia greatly.

"I need your help, both of you. I've hired a truck next Saturday, but I need help moving. You know I'm now retired from being Director of Nurses here. I've decided to move to Chemainus, a place I've always loved. Two of my girlfriends who've settled there recently say it's a great place to live. I have an uncle there, too."

Amelia called to her husband, who was having coffee and reading the paper in the living room. "What are we doing next Saturday, Jean Paul? Margaret needs our help. She's moving to Chemainus!"

"What time does she want us to be there?" He shouted back, folding up his newspaper and heading on his way to the kitchen.

He took the phone from Amelia and said, "Hi, Margaret, of course we'll be there. We've bought a new truck, so we'll be a great help, you lucky girl!" "Is that half Native, half Frenchman going to be there with you?" He teased.

Margaret had struck up a very interesting relationship with a man who carved totem poles among other sculptures of different mediums. He was now famous for his bronze figures of early First Nation's heroes, both Canadian and American. These statues in action were featured in several art magazines, and were on display in the Victoria museum. The huge one he has been working on in the United States is ongoing.

Margaret explained that she had the Nanaimo end covered for loading the rented truck but needed help when they got to Chemainus, to unload and to fix everything up in the house she rented there.

"And yes, Jean Paul, Rene will be with me for part of the whole move. I have friends helping me in Nanaimo, and I will drive the truck down to Chemainus."

A week later the couple met Margaret at her new address. Margaret was already there working with her new friend, Rene Tohonnie (Tohonnie means clan near the water.)

Rene was not a tall man; he measured about five foot eight or nine, had long dark hair combed straight back, which fell to his shoulders. He had removed his soft beige leather jacket to expose very muscular arms, a straight strong back and wide shoulders. He turned to face Margaret; he smiled a shy smile, which lit up his oval face, and handsome features. His large dark eyes revealed a man of gentle nature.

Amelia, Jean Paul, and Rene got right to work unloading the boxes and carrying them into the house. Margaret directed them as to where to place the boxes that she had carefully labelled.

"Oh my goodness!" Margaret exclaimed as Rene carried the last box of dishes into the kitchen. He had placed it on top of a box marked Pots and Pans. As he turned away to fetch more, he hit the box of dishes slightly with his hip and Margaret watched helplessly from the doorway as "Aunt Nellies dishes" slid off the pile and fell in a dull thump to the floor.

"I hope those antique dishes of aunt Nellie's didn't break! She left them to me before she died" Margaret rushed over, almost in tears. Aunt Nellie had been very important in her early years.

"Never mind, Margo Ajei (Ajei means my heart, one that signifies great importance) Little one, we will buy you some wonderful new ones, or I'll make some out of the clay I found close to the town," Rene reassured her in a soothing tone as he put a strong arm around her.

She looked up at him suspiciously, then gave a big sigh, and asked, "How long will it take you to make a whole set?"

He shrugged, and hugged her closer "I'm hoping we'll have the rest of our lives together, but if you want dishes right away, maybe we'll ask my friend, Luke, the local potter here for some new ones." He smiled down on her again, warmly.

"You loved his work didn't you? Eh bien, I'll speak to him tomorrow. Let's have a glass of wine together, no? Then we'll open Auntie Nellie's box and see if there's damage."

She sighed, leaning against him in comfort.

"Well, maybe it just fell and nothing's broke. Yes, let's first assess the damage with auntie Nellie's dishes. Maybe there'll be enough to keep. But I sure liked those dishes that Luke was selling."

"Did auntie Nellie cook good meals? Are her dishes big and strong and will hold lots of food?" He asked, adding "Like Luke's?"

Jean Paul hid a big grin behind his hand as he set the legs back on the kitchen table and righted it. Amelia caught the twinkle in his eye and his nod at Rene.

Two conspirators, she thought as she watched them working together. *Next thing I know, Rene will be borrowing my motorcycle and the two of them will take off in a cloud of dust!*

The girls were setting up Margaret's bed and arranging the furniture in the bedroom when the men came upstairs to help. Rene pointed at the single bed and asked, "Margo! I didn't know this was the spare room! Are you expecting a niece or someone to visit?"

"No," she answered quietly. "Rene, this is my bed." He took a deep breath in. His facial expression changed, now portraying incredulous amazement, then shock before it assumed dead pan. He turned his face away, wide-eyed and muttered to himself, *So that's why* as he went outside to carry in more boxes. Jean Paul coughed, and went outside to join him.

It was becoming rapidly apparent that Rene definitely had his own ideas, and that sleeping in a single bed was not one of them.

When the men returned with more boxes, Margaret said softly, "Rene, thanks for helping me so much, I am grateful for all your help."

She looked as if she would burst into tears.

He put his cardboard box down, went to Margaret, cupped her face in his strong hands, kissed her gently on her forehead and said quietly, "I understand completely little one." He added quietly, "Margo, sweet little thing, you are the only girl in my own heart! But I do have wonderful plans for both of us." He kissed her softly again, then turned to get more boxes.

Amelia, who was bent over putting things into drawers, giggled, and glanced at Margaret to see her reaction.

Margaret was blushing, helplessly, and looked very sad. She didn't seem to know how to respond.

This is going to be very interesting in the next few weeks, thought Jean Paul. "*We'll have to keep a sharp eye on both of them.*"

"Let's go eat," suggested Amelia. "I saw a nice restaurant on the main drag last time we were here."

"Good idea" agreed her husband. It'll be my treat for all of us," he said gesturing to Margaret and Rene.

At lunch, Margaret and Rene seemed to regain their sense of humour, and soon were quipping back and forth about how they had met, all the fun they had in the short time they had known each other. They asked Amelia and Jean Paul about their time of romance before getting married. Soon, many funny stories were traded back and forth; the laughter grew louder and louder until the manager came over with the bill, asking quietly if there was anything else before they left.

Rene invited Amelia and Jean Paul to come and see what he was working on in his studio. Amelia suggested they drop her and Margaret off to continue setting things straight in the house. "We'll come and see your work next time, Rene."

When the girls were back in Margaret's new home, and alone to talk 'girl talk', Margaret confessed she had fallen in love with this artist-carver, Rene. She said he had settled in Chemainus recently, originally from the USA. Margaret said he was from the Navajo tribe. In 1942, during the war, the army had requested him to join a group of fellow Navajo soldiers. They all spoke both English and Navajo well. The army called them the Code Talkers.

She said he had explained to her that often the men had worked behind enemy lines speaking only Navajo to their partners outside the area, as they described the terrain and enemy encampment. They were commended for their bravery, and were well respected by the other soldiers. Their code was declassified this year, which upset Rene. Theirs was the only code that had never been broken by the enemy.

He said, "It is not a code. It is our language."

"Amelia, I never thought I would meet anyone I could love like I love this man!"

Amelia listened quietly and offered nothing but a warm listening ear and a thoughtful quiet reception to her words.

When Margaret asked Amelia what she thought of the carver, Amelia said, "It's hard to say what I think right now, Margaret. He has a good sense of humour, seems very attracted to you, and is not afraid to work. He also seems like a very kind and intuitive man, and he wants to take care of you; that's obvious. The important thing Margaret, is what do you think of him?"

"I like the way he creates beautiful art. It's like he works a figure through its soul."

She smiled almost dreamily. "He is thoughtful of me; he doesn't have any addictions; he's educated, went to trade school then had a chance for university and took it. Before he retired to sculpt full-time he taught in a high school and loved his students. They reciprocated that love by getting excellent marks and going on in education. Many of them were Native Americans, but there were some Native Canadians, too. They still come to see him."

She got up and poured two cups of coffee, and fixed them up with cream. "His mother is Native is father French Canadian. They were never married. He took his mother's last name, and loves her very much. His home here is beautiful, close to the water, and well-built of logs. He stripped the logs himself, then hired a contractor. They worked together to build it the way he wanted. You've noticed he doesn't hold back in saying what he thinks. I kinda like that about him, but I guess I'm used to 'being in charge' and it rattles me a bit."

"Let's have one more coffee while we talk and then get back to work. Where's the linen for your bed?"

"I think it's on the bottom of that pile of boxes over there, "she said pointing at several piled boxes. "It's marked on the side, 'Linen'."

"Well let's get at it. Otherwise, you may get an invitation to a bigger bed than you expect."

"You know what, Amelia, I wouldn't mind that. But I have to confess something. I'll bet you didn't know it. And I've never told Rene yet. I'm still a virgin."

Amelia sat down with a solid thump, and an astonished expression on her face.

"Holy smokes, Margaret, let's get your bed made right now. You'll need a real education, and at our age, a big tube of lubricant ready handy for when 'that time' comes around." Amelia got up and started moving the boxes to access the linen box.

"This Native American-Frenchman means business! Margo, little one, you had better see a doctor right soon, and be ready when that time comes." She added, "And maybe explain to him sometime, like as soon as possible. Otherwise he may think you're rejecting him."

The house was put into a relatively tidy order by the time Jean Paul and Amelia left. The newest Chemainus resident was tired but happy. When Rene suggested that he return the following day, she happily sent him off with a big 'Thank you' for all you've done," a happy hug and kiss.

Amelia and Jean Paul discussed the day as they drove on their way home.

"Sweetheart, there's something that's troubling to me. It's about Margaret and Rene." Jean Paul held up one hand to interrupt.

"Don't bother your head, my love. Rene saw the single bed and figured it out right away. He's a real good guy. He'll take his time. He loves her very much."

CHAPTER 32

FROM THE JOURNAL OF MARGARET TAHOONIE, APRIL 15, 1969

MY GOODNESS, I DIDN'T KNOW A WOMAN LIKE ME COULD feel so much happiness. Since I married Rene, my life has taken such a wonderful turn.

Every day I'm dancing on clouds.

Life here in Chemainus is more than blissful. Words do not describe my feelings.

Let me tell you about this little British Columbian town. It was a logging town from 1858. There were many First Nations people living in the Cowichan Valley, and Chemainus was originally named "Tsa-meen-is", which means broken chest. The history of that name came about because a powerful shaman had survived a massive chest wound, and became the band's chief of the Stz'uminus tribe. In 1880, the railroad came through Chemainus bringing workers from China and Japan to work along the railway, and also to work in the lumber industry."

My goodness, it is already April 15th 1969 and here I am getting involved in Chemainus and forgetting to write all about the folks I've been telling you about in this book!

Here's the latest on Amelia and Jean Paul, as well as all the others I know in this story. In case you've forgotten, Jean Paul and Amelia rode up to see me in Chemainus yesterday in their new truck. They brought their motorcycles, too, so they could wander about and see the sights, they said. Jean Paul calls them bikes.

Those two seemed quite comfortable and happy riding together. I might also say I thought of them riding happily into the sunset as I watched them ride off to explore everything in Chemainus.

You know, the feeling I got watching them was the same as when I watched those old cowboy pictures when we were kids. It's obvious they are deeply, happily in love. I'm glad for both of them. They told me of another trip they want to take going back to Peru. Jean Paul wanted them to go on their bikes but after investigating what life in Peru and South America some-times involves, they decided to take a longer tour, and go by plane. Apparently, even the poorest person from Canada is considered rich by some S.A. standards.

Amelia has lent Rene her motorcycle the odd time he and Jean Paul can see more of the country while Amelia and I have a nice coffee and chat.

She and Jean Paul both have good jobs. Amelia still works for that lawyer, and the University of Victoria hired Jean Paul several years ago for their program on the environment. They are both doing very well, and have bought their own house, the one they were renting initially, and seem very, very happy.

Dr. Otto and Hilda took a cruise to Alaska, but he had another heart attack and had to be flown back to the Royal Jubilee. He didn't last long after that. Hilda still keeps tabs on what is hap-pening in Happy Days Retirement Home, and is busy being a volunteer there.

Karla told me all about her husband Adam's new office as well as little Ben's progress. Adam has built up a private practice helping people sort out their problems. He's a full-fledged psychologist, and also does contract work in the hospitals. Oh, did I tell you that little Ben isn't little anymore? He's shot up and is the tallest in his class. He rides his bike everywhere and delivers papers at five in the morning. Imagine! Then he goes to his basketball practice at seven. Everyone is so proud of him. He won the contest for all the school kids in art, put on by the provincial government. Guess what he did with the money he won? He opened a bank account to help him go to art school in Vancouver. He also donated his painting to the home. He said that he started being a true artist when he got lessons from Amelia. Betty Armstrong told me she and Dr. Allan Gregory are planning a wedding and they want me to be part of it. Honestly, it feels like spring has sprung and all the birds and animals (and I guess some of the humans) are getting ready to make love and babies.

I talked to Karl Jr. who is still treasurer for Happy Days Retirement Home, besides owning his own accounting business in Victoria.

The older Karl, the dad, seems to have set new goals for himself. After taking flying lessons, he was hired by Air Canada and is flying almost everywhere around the world. His wife left him after the addiction episode, and Karl seems to be having a wonderful time with some movie star he's been seeing.

I heard from Jean Paul about the two boys who rescued him after the accident. They both have graduated and are on their way. Hans, the one who fixed his bike as one of his school projects, has opened his own Repair shop. He's a specialist in repairing motorcycles as well as cars. Bikers are coming to him from all over BC and Alberta. Craig, the one who was in medical school, is now specializing in bone surgery at Victoria General.

Remember Lori, the nurse's aide, who helped Amelia so much when Amelia first entered Happy Day's Retirement Home? Lori

graduated from the school of Recreation Therapy and is doing a
wonderful job keeping the residents active and interested in life.
They go on bus trips, sometimes up here to Chemainus…to see
what our Indigenous carvers are doing. Happy Days Retirement
Home is running at full capacity. The board has decided to add
another wing. They now have people in the home who fit into
three categories. The first category is for the ones who can care
for themselves mostly, but need a suite to live in and a staff who
will give them two meals a day. These people prepare their own
breakfasts and do their own laundry. (Something like living in a
resort but having the staff to help them if they need help.) They
call it "Independent Living". The second category is for people
who need some care, some medical attention but are ambula-
tory and capable of attending the activities provided by the new
Recreation Department. They call that "Assisted Living".

The new wing at Happy Days is going to house the people who
need total care or are dying. They call that wing of the new building, "Total Care," and another part of that wing is called "Hospice"
There, they give Palliative Care. I've heard some residents say that
once they have come to Happy Days Retirement Home they have
finally come home.

Hilda, Dr. Otto's wife, said she knows Otto is a very happy
man about how everything has turned out. Apparently Otto
said if he died before he was ready (his heart gave him a lot of
trouble in his last days) he would be checking on us all to see if
we behaved. Hilda gave a big dinner for all of us. She thanked us
all for our interest and help in Happy Days Retirement Home.
She said the home has become a truly happy place for its residents. She gave a great speech at the fundraising event the board
threw for the public. All donations and the money they charged
would go towards putting up that new wing. The plans show it's a
beautiful hospice wing with all the newest equipment.

Amelia's kids seem to be producing babies at a great rate. She and Jean Paul now have seven grandchildren. Apparently, there are more on the way.

Those two boys, Amelia's sons, who were working in Alberta? They made some good money, then left for Ontario. They bought out a car dealer, and are selling Mazda cars imported from Japan.

They both have been married several years now and are doing real well. They fly back and forth to visit Amelia and Jean Paul.

Life goes on, happiness and adversity play hop scotch throughout, making us wiser with our growing maturity.

Jean Paul is a good grandfather to all the children. He has a real good singing voice, as does Amelia. They are welcome at many people's parties as well as the church they attend. He's taught us family and friends and the older kids many French songs. At our family parties, we sing and dance, as he says, " like we do in Quebec." We always have a great time when Jean Paul's around.

The home also hired a dietician and the food is both delicious as well as good for the residents. I'm telling you all, life has taken a very positive note since we began this saga, so many years ago.

All in all, the many trials that occurred as this book unfolded have been overcome. I firmly believe all trauma and trials bring their own gifts of wisdom and experience. I'm sure there are more problems occurring as I write this, that's life, isn't it? Problems only emerge for us to overcome and sometimes are a result of someone's or our own questionable choices. Eventually, we learn to avoid them on our quest to grow and mature

Life is good, and we will survive anything that comes along with the love of God, family, and friends. We grow upwards, becoming better people as we learn wisdom and patience on our journeys.

What more can a person ask?

CPSIA information can be obtained
at www.ICGtesting.com
Printed in the USA
LVOW10s0139130517
534373LV00001B/1/P

9 781773 023090